CLAIMED BY NOATAK

A STEAMY ALIEN ROMANCE

GALACTIC PIRATE BRIDES

BOOK THREE

TAMSIN LEY

Twin Leaf Press

Cover by The Book Brander

Paperback version
ISBN-13: 978-1-950027-01-9
Copyright © 2018 Twin Leaf Press
All rights reserved.

Twin Leaf Press
PO Box 672255
Chugiak, AK 99567

Chapter One

Marlis leveled her Blackstar E-11 and squeezed the trigger. The target at the end of the range flashed three times. *Bulls-eye.*

"Fuck them and their standards," she muttered, pushing the target back another meter. She took aim and fired several more shots, each one flashing success. The E-11 zero-recoil pulse pistol had been a gift for her eleventh birthday, and after fourteen years and many other weapons, it was still her favorite. "I was even on time this morning."

"Good shot, Marlis!" Marlis's AI chimed from her wrist-band. The artificial intelligence was supposed to assist Marlis with anger management and lapses in memory, but its trite encouragements did nothing to assuage her today.

"Shut up, Twerp." Marlis racked the energy coil's cooling module and set the pistol aside. Picking up her customized Renegade MCS6 rifle, she reset the target for long-range and sighted in.

The lanes of the Syndicorp cruiser's firing range were all occupied today, but she had eyes only for her target, imagining each bulls-eye as the face of the service recruiter assigned to her file. *I'm legacy, for fuck's sake.* Descended from a long line of trooper personnel with excellent records. And it wasn't as if she couldn't keep up during the drills. She could out-shoot, out-run, and out-wrestle every woman as well as most men in the squad. So what if she needed a little help to remember what day it was?

"Marlis!" a man's voice barked behind her.

Gut tightening, she whipped the rifle around.

Her father's narrow gaze flicked to the barrel, his mouth in a grim line as she lowered the weapon.

She refused to feel any regret about being battle-ready. Mom had died while she and Marlis had been on Pulati for a mother-daughter vacation. Ten-year-old Marlis had only survived the sudden terrorist outbreak by hiding beneath her mother's dead body for sixteen hours.

Marlis had no intention of letting her guard down. Ever.

Dad crossed his arms over his chest, covering the service ribbons on the lapel of his uniform. "You missed your date last night."

"That's tonight." Even as she said it, she realized she was probably wrong.

Twerp's feminine voice rose from her wrist strap. "I informed you of the engagement at seventeen hundred yesterday and again at seventeen twenty. You said you were in no mood to give someone a blow job and directed me not to remind you again."

Marlis's face heated to match the rising flush in her father's usually pallid cheeks. When would she ever remember to put in her earbud? Teeth clenched, she grated out, "Shut up, Twerp."

Dad squared his shoulders, looking Marlis straight in the eye. "He's a respectable young man, Marlis. From a good family. You couldn't ask for a better match."

"I don't want a better match. I want to join the troopers." She turned around and took aim at the target once more. "Get me a date with someone useful and I'll go."

"I can't rebuild the bridges you burn fast enough."

Refusing to be distracted, she let out a slow breath and squeezed the trigger in rapid succession. The target lit up on all but the final shot. She lowered the rifle. "I'd be a good soldier, Dad."

A gentle hand settled on her shoulder. "You blew up at your recruiter."

Marlis fuzzily remembered her rage at the small-eyed, beak-nosed recruiter who oversaw the drills the troopers used to weed out unworthy candidates. He was supposed to test the recruits' physical aptitudes. Instead, he'd thrown history questions at them. She seemed to recall a lot of swear words coming out of her mouth instead of answers. "What good is a history lesson going to do for me on the battle field?"

"He thinks you're a liability. They want to rescind your weapon carry permit." Dad's voice lowered with unaccustomed softness. "I'm sorry."

His words felt like a punch in the gut. Give up her pistol? *No way.* No longer able to focus on the target, Marlis shoved the E-11 into the holster built into the back hip of her pants and shouldered her rifle, turning to leave.

"Marlis."

She continued walking.

"Marlis. Your rifle case."

Face on fire, she halted; she might still have a permit to carry, but exiting the range actually welding a weapon, even on a military ship, was a big no-no. *Stupid memory.* Other AI models came equipped with a visual node to track items, but Marlis's therapist claimed that requiring her to remember some things on her own would help her improve.

Squaring her shoulders, she spun on her heel and retrieved the case, visually verifying there was nothing else she was leaving behind. Her father's watchful gaze made Marlis doubt herself. What else was she forgetting? *Dammit!*

Reacting to her elevated heart rate, Twerp vibrated against her wrist, encouraging her to remain calm, then came to the rescue with a reminder. "Marlis, you are scheduled for lunch with your sister in forty-three minutes. May I remind you that Attie is routinely early?"

"Thank you, Twerp." She offered her dad a weak smile. "I need to go clean up. I'll talk to you later."

Passing uniformed personnel as she moved through the carrier's corridors, Marlis silently repeated her mantra from years in therapy; *there is no danger.* Yet it was a hard mantra to believe when she'd just been told her right to carry a firearm was in jeopardy. She switched to *anger does more harm than good.* By the time she reached the family housing section and the modest quarters she shared with her dad and sister, Twerp had stopped buzzing.

She stowed her rifle and washed her face, then headed toward the mess hall on the lower deck where Attie probably already waited. Her big sister had been accepted into the troopers over a year ago, quickly rising to Private First Class. The job left Attie little time to visit with family, although she made a point of having lunch weekly with Marlis. No matter how routine it might be, Marlis's heart lightened at the thought of seeing her.

Uniform crisp and ash-blonde hair trimmed to short ringlets, Attie was already seated at their usual table. The huge room echoed with the predominantly human lunch crowd filling long tables, the homogeny interspersed by a few clusters of aliens. Attie's head was down, eyes scanning the screen of a polycom as Marlis approached. A new gold chevron adorned the epaulet on her shoulder.

"You made corporal?" Marlis asked, unable to drag her gaze from the emblem.

Attie set the polycom aside and rose, brushing her fingertips over the rank badge before rounding the table to give Marlis a hug. "I officially got the promotion today."

"Hugging's against regulation. They're gonna come take that chevron back." Marlis squeezed her sister, trying to summon a sense of humor instead of jealousy. Her sister was so together.

Attie rolled her eyes and once more took her seat. She glanced toward the long chow line. "You want to go first while I finish these reports?"

Nodding, Marlis got in line among the uniformed personnel. Prior to this moment, she'd always strutted into the mess hall knowing she was among her people; it was only a matter of time before she had her own uniform. Now it felt like everyone's eyes were on her; challenging her worth.

Putting two plates onto her tray, she selected the chicken curry and skipped the dessert section, opting for two coffees with cream instead. Although Attie never asked, Marlis always came back with food for both of them. It seemed like a waste of precious sister-time to send Attie to stand in line all over again.

Returning to the table, Marlis set both plates down. "It was this or something that looked like cat vomit."

"Thanks." Attie picked up her fork and poked at a sliced tomato, edging it away from her chicken. "How're things with Dad?"

Something about the set of Attie's shoulders had Marlis on edge. "He's still trying to set me up with Colonel Yan's son. Why do you ask?"

Attie shrugged. "Is he cute?"

Now Marlis's warning bells began to chime. "Some people think so. Why?"

Taking a big bite, Attie chewed slowly before answering. "You turn twenty-six soon. You know what that means."

Of course she knew. At twenty-six, she'd lose her status as her father's dependent and all the perks that came with it. Unless she joined the troopers herself, she'd be sent to ground, forced to join the civilians on one muddy planet or another. Trapped, just like on Pulati. *Never, never, never.* "Of course I do. What does that have to do with Colonel Yan's son?"

"A lot of people enjoy marriage. It'd give you a partner."

"Marrying some douche bag I could beat at arm wrestling won't solve my problems."

Attie tapped her fork against her plate nervously. "Marlis, you need someone you can rely on."

"What do you mean? I have you. And I have Dad when he's not being a dick."

Setting her fork down, Attie took a deep breath, gaze locked with Marlis's. "I've been assigned to the flagship *Icarus.*"

It felt as if someone had just opened the ship's blast doors, sucking away all the oxygen. Marlis's vision narrowed, the room fading around her. *Attie can't leave.* Her sister was her rock. The one person she could always turn to. Twerp buzzed almost painfully against her skin, telling her to calm down.

Attie leaned forward, speaking slowly. "It's part of my promotion. A great opportunity for advancement. I'll be serving on Admiral Olly's primary staff."

Marlis gulped. "I don't see you enough as it is."

"It'll be okay." Attie reached across the table and covered Marlis's hand with hers. "We can still talk on the vid. And Dad says—" She cut off, biting a corner of her lip as if she'd said too much.

"You told Dad already?" Marlis choked out. She'd always been Attie's confidante, the first to hear anything. "Before me?"

"He's worried about you, Marlis. You're his baby. He even called James."

Their older brother, James, had left when Marlis was ten, before she'd gone to Pulati with Mom. He was currently a Staff Sergeant on Aleigh. "What does James have to do with me?"

"He's trying to get you a dependency waiver. It's easier on planetary bases."

"You mean live with James?" Marlis shot to her feet, her blood on fire. "You're kidding me!" People at surrounding tables turned to stare. Twerp vibrated doggedly against her wrist. Still, Marlis couldn't keep her voice down. "And you agree with him?"

"No." Attie kept level contact with Marlis's eyes, exuding confidence. "Sit down, please."

"There is no danger, Marlis," Twerp added.

"Shut the fuck up, Twerp." There *was* danger. It was all around her, from places she never expected. "Dad says they're going to take away my weapon carry permit."

"What? They can't!" Attie's calm demeanor broke, and she rose to her feet.

Oddly enough, that made Marlis feel better. "I had an argument with my recruiter." Heat filled her face, and she lowered herself slowly back to her seat, scrubbing a hand over her forehead. "Do you think they'll let me petition for another try?"

Attie sighed, looking down at her little sister a moment before shaking her head no. "I won't lie to you. I've heard talk that you're unstable."

For the first time she could remember, Marlis felt tears prick her eyes. Actual, honest-to-god tears. She hated it. "What am I going to do?"

Picking up the polycom beside her plate, Attie began tapping in commands. "Since you can't live on board the carrier after your birthday and you don't want to live with James," she set the device on the tabletop and shoved it toward Marlis, "I think you should look for a job."

Marlis stared at the polycom, her pulse thundering in her ears. *A job?* As in something other than working for the troopers? Her brain refused to transform the blocks of text on the screen into meaningful information. "What is this?"

"Ads for jobs on Whylon Station. There are other options for you than military service. Legit shipping businesses looking for hired guns. Bodyguards. That kind of thing."

"Not through the troopers?" Marlis frowned. "Don't companies contract through the corp for those services?"

Her sister laughed and retrieved the polycom. "There's a world outside of Syndicorp—whole regions of the galaxy, in fact. Not everyone can afford troopers. You're fantastic with weapons, Sis. And you want to protect people. Let's find a way for you to do it." Attie stood. "I have to go or I'll be late for duty. I forwarded you the info." She took a few steps away, then looked over her shoulder and winked. "Oh, and don't tell Dad I suggested this, okay? I'd like to keep my reputation as the good daughter."

Watching her sister's retreating back, Marlis repeated her mantra. *There is no danger.* Yet she couldn't manage to take a full breath, let alone pull out her own polycom. *Work other than with the service?*

"Would you like me to assist?" Twerp asked calmly.

Grateful for any help she could get, Marlis nodded. "Yeah. Tell me about these shipping companies."

Chapter Two

Noatak strode along the *Hardship's* corridor toward the cargo hold where Joy, the First Mate of the *Kinship*, was waiting in the shuttle. They were headed to Whylon Station to meet women who wanted to join their Resistance. *Resistance.* He grimaced as he walked. He still had his doubts about Joy's documentary attracting the right kind of people, but with both ships' captains off on a mission, that left him and Joy in charge of the interviews.

As he passed the med bay, Mek stepped out and held up a hand. "Before you go, we need to talk."

"I don't have time." Noatak scowled and shoved the medic's hand out of the way. It was enough he that could feel his ionic powers weakening every day; he didn't need to be hovered over like a newly hatched kemeg.

Mek trotted alongside him as he continued walking. "You need to strap into a nav-grav seat for the trip to Whylon Station."

That stopped Noatak cold. He spun on his heel to face the doctor. "No way. Nav-grav is for wimps."

"Your ionic levels dropped another six percent since my last scan." Mek pulled the med scanner from his belt and pulled up Noatak's record. "I ran some models, and it's only a matter of time before your secondary heart gives out completely."

"I strap in and Joy will know something's up. Soon as she knows, everyone will. Last thing I need is the entire universe knowing I'm weak."

"Let me put this into terms you'll understand." Mek lowered the scanner and focused on Noatak. "If you keep using your ionic powers, even for small things, you could die."

"Could is a lot different from will." Noatak rolled his shoulders. He'd faced death many times. But he'd always imagined going out in a blaze of glory, not dying from ionic failure like an old man. "Besides, aren't you looking into some procedure to fix me?"

"I am, but there isn't a lot of research available on denaidan physiology, especially with what's left of our planet under quarantine." The Termination had not only killed all females of their species, it'd also poisoned their home world beyond repair; no one had set foot on Denaida-daru in over fifteen years. Mek shook his head, lips pressed into a thin line. "Until I can determine a course of action, I recommend no shielding, no sensing enemy heartbeats, and definitely no burn without a nav-grav seat."

"What the fuck good am I for our cause if I can't do any of that?" Noatak crossed his arms. "Next, you'll tell me not to ping the women I'm about to interview." The applicants were going to join the pirates not only as crew, but potentially as mates; it was vital he select ones who would also be receptive to the nanites.

"Unfortunately, yes." Mek's stoic face softened. He opened his mouth as if to say more, then shut it again.

Noatak narrowed his eyes. Mek was usually abrupt. If he was holding back, it must be bad. "What else?"

Mek looked down, mouth pursed. "If these women accept the nanites, you'll need to avoid sexual activity."

The news was like a physical blow. They were about to bring a female crew onto the ship—the first ever—and he was being told not to touch? *Ellam Cua.* His voice rose like a growl from deep inside his chest. "You're serious?"

"During sexual climax, your secondary heart automatically engages—"

"I don't need an anatomy lesson, doc. I get it." He let out a sigh, thinking about soft skin and pliant mouths and all the things he and the other denaidans had been dreaming about for fifteen years. Before the discovery of the nanites, non-denaidan females died during sex. Now it might be him. He rubbed his bearded chin. "Might be worth it, though."

Mek's eyes narrowed. "It's not only you at stake in that scenario, you know. If a mate bond were to form, you'd make her a widow before she even understood what was happening."

Noatak felt the blood drain from his face. He hadn't thought of that. Not every sexual encounter created a mate bond, but when it did happen, the bond was for life.

Mek put a consoling hand on his shoulder. "I'm sorry. I'll keep working on a fix."

Noatak shrugged the hand away, every muscle in his body tight. "I'd better go."

"Noatak," Mek called, but Noatak didn't slow down.

Numb from the shock, Noatak reached the cargo bay and climbed aboard the small craft, going through the motions for takeoff automatically. He settled into the pilot's seat next to Joy, unable to look at her—female, mated, a partner for Kashatok in every sense of the word. Noatak would never know what that felt like. *That'll teach you to hope.*

"You okay?" Joy asked, the camera in her eye dilating as she adjusted her filters to look at him. Filming, as usual.

"Yup." He flicked the controls to close the hatch and initiate the launch. "Have everything you need?"

She reached overhead and pulled the nav-grav harness over her head and shoulders. "I think so. There are a surprising number of people interested in the Resistance."

After being called a pirate for fifteen years, he doubted the general population would stop thinking of them as criminals just because they adopted a new name. "Or they just want to gawk at some real pirates. How many are we interviewing this time?"

"Eight or so. Some may bring friends."

He grunted in response, privately hoping there were a bunch of no-shows. After Mek's little talk, he wasn't thrilled about interviewing a bunch of women he could never touch.

Signaling the cargo bay doors to open, he maneuvered the craft out into space and began programming the burn frequency to jump to Whylon Station. The shuttle cleared the *Hardship's* perimeter, and he hovered a finger over the button to engage the burn drive. He glanced at Joy. No fucking way was he strapping in. Even a human could endure a short burn cycle without shielding. He'd have a killer headache and fatigue, but that was nothing new. "Engaging burn."

Before he could second-guess himself, he hit the button.

CHAPTER THREE

Fuming, Marlis waited at Whylon Station's public IGC booth, watching the finofan ahead of her extend and retract his ear fans as he spoke to the comm screen. He finished, and she barely let him escape the booth before pushing inside. The hard plastic seat was still warm from his backside, and the interior of the booth smelled like moldy lettuce, but she didn't care. She was going to murder her father.

Hours ago, she'd strutted into her first interview full of confidence. Attie'd set everything up, from the time and place of the meeting to information about the owner. Getting a job should've been a cakewalk. Instead, the portly owner had told her they were no longer looking for help. The receptionist at the second interview smiled condescendingly, patted her hand, and told her they didn't want any trouble with the law. By the time she walked into the offices of the third shipping company and the flushed young man at the desk told her she should call home, she'd pulled up her seldom-used charm and asked why not. Flushing even more, he'd shown her his polycom.

On her profile at a social media site she'd abandoned years ago, her face now appeared with the word MISSING and contact information for her father. She'd only set the account up because her therapist thought it would be good for her to interact with friends, but Marlis had no interest in pretending to like people's baby pictures and stupid quotes. Apparently, potential employers checked these sites and must've contacted Dad.

Scanning her credit chip, she punched in the code and waited for Dad to answer. The moment his pallid face appeared on-screen, she leaned forward. "How could you?"

He didn't bat an eyelash, as if he'd been expecting her call. "Come home now, Marlis. I'm making arrangements for you to have a job here."

"I could've had my pick of jobs here, except for your interference!" Marlis's blood was boiling, and the incessant thrum of Twerp's vibration against her wrist had all but numbed her hand. "What did you tell them?"

"You can barely remember to tie your shoes, Marlis. You're not ready to be out on your own. It's not your fault, considering what happened to your mother. Syndicorp's military division owes you for that. They owe us all. I'm going to make sure they take care of you."

She ground her teeth. "By take care of me, you mean let me push papers or scrub toilets for the other soldiers. No, thank you."

"Now, Marlis, everyone has to earn a living, and you can't be good at everything."

"I'm good at wielding a gun, Dad. Get me a job doing that."

"You've never been on your own. You have no idea what kinds of trouble you can get into."

"I'd be fine if you'd just let me."

"If you were going to school, maybe, or taking a retail position in a reputable establishment. But becoming a hired gun is ludicrous. I don't know why your sister would've suggested it."

"Because she knows it's the only thing I'm good at. The only thing I want to do." The little amber light at the corner of the comm screen began blinking that her time was nearly up, requesting more credits to continue.

Dad shook his head, frowning. "Come home and we'll discuss your options. I love you, Marlis. I only want you safe."

The burning in Marlis's gut was making her feel like she was about to spew acid all over the screen. She loved her dad, loved her family. But the one-way ticket to the station had cost her nearly her entire savings—which wasn't much, since she'd spent almost every dime she collected on weapon upgrades. If she went back now, she might never make it off the Syndicorp carrier again. The comm light shifted to red for the final ten-second warning.

"I'm staying here. Talk to you later, Dad." She ended the call and swung out of the booth, shouldering past the others waiting in line. She paused in the middle of the teeming corridor, drawing a blank on which direction to turn.

Ever-helpful, Twerp chirped from her wrist, "Do you wish to return to the hostel, Marlis?"

"Sure." Where else was she going to go? Her feet felt heavy as she considered how she was going to keep paying for a bunk without a job, let alone the rental for the weapons locker. The station frowned upon average citizens tromping around with MCS6's and pulse cartridges, although she'd kept her E-11 holstered beneath her waistband.

"Turn left," Twerp advised.

Marlis began trekking through the crowd, then changed her mind and shifted course toward a nearby cantina. Maybe a drink would settle her nerves.

Entering the bar, she passed a massive yanipa-nimayu bouncer kicked back on four of his six massive legs. One of his four eyes shifted to her holster, but he didn't stop her from passing. Inside, a sign flickered over the central bar—The Junk Heap. The soles of her shoes clung to the tacky floor, and the herbal stink of cirripi weed drifted from the back. Two human servers flitted among the scattered booths and high tables.

As Marlis looked for a seat, Twerp piped up over the music wailing from speakers in the ceiling, "I have taken the liberty of accessing the station's want ads and can locate no advertisements for guards or weapons specialists. Would you like me to look for alternate employment opportunities?"

On the barstool next to her, a thin man with grease-stained fingers looked at her from the corner of his eye, gaze flitting to her wrist before returning his attention to the bubbling drink in front of him. He was seedy, but not a threat, and Marlis settled onto her stool before lifting her wrist close to her mouth. "Not so loud, Twerp. Geez."

She'd forgotten her earbud on the carrier and didn't have the time or money to get a new one at the moment. Not that she ever remembered to wear it, anyway. She signaled the posungi bartender, who waggled his bright orange facial tentacles in her direction to indicate he'd be right there. While she waited, she spoke toward her wrist in a low voice. "Twerp, do any of the independent vessels post ads with the station? If I can't get a job with the shipping companies, maybe I can freelance."

"Checking."

The guy next to her looked at her again. "You'd be better off searching the boards." He lifted his chin toward the far wall. "Though a good-looking gal like you might make more money on her back than on a ship."

Marlis reconsidered her assessment of him, but when he shrugged and turned back to his drink, she decided her first guess had been right. Looking over her shoulder toward where he'd gestured, she spotted a bulletin board covered in haggard scraps of paper near the restrooms.

"How archaic," she muttered as she headed toward them. All manner of languages covered the pages, some typed, some scrawled. The few she could read in Corporate Common were selling items or services and one ad for a room rental. There were even two posters she could only assume were Cartel, offering bounties for information about a dark-haired woman and her brother. As she was attempting to decipher a splotchy note requesting someone willing to perform a sexual position she'd never heard of, an argument broke out near the restroom door.

"I said you mistook my words." A petite woman around Marlis's age was jerking ineffectually against the grip of a human male who looked like he'd taken one too many puffs of cirripi. "Just let me go."

"C'mon, baby, I just want to talk." He grinned, exposing a dead front tooth.

Marlis didn't like the way his fingers clamped around the woman's upper arm. She took a single step toward them, her right hand tensed to whip out her pistol if need be. "Everything okay?"

The brunette shook her head fiercely enough to bounce her curls, her wide eyes full of alarm. "No."

"Back off, Blondie," said the man with barely a look toward Marlis. "You ain't my type."

Marlis wasn't particularly good at hand-to-hand combat, preferring the sure results her E-11 provided, but she'd had some training. Lightning quick, she reached out and twisted the man's grip free of the woman's arm. The man fell to his knees. "Ow! What the fuck, woman?"

Pathetic. Not even worth getting angry over. She leaned in close enough to smell his reeking, weed-tainted breath. "She asked you to let her go. Now get out of here before I call that bouncer over there. Unless you think he'll be more polite?"

He pulled his arm against his chest the moment she let go, his hateful gaze still on her face. But she could tell he wasn't the type to put up a fight. Most likely he'd slink off to lick his wounds until he found another easy target.

The smaller woman watched the man scramble upright and retreat out the door, then extended a hand to Marlis. "Thank you. My name's Emmy."

"Marlis." Marlis accepted the handshake.

"Let me buy you a drink." Emmy adjusted her blouse hem around her plump hips. "It's the least I can do."

Marlis shrugged. "I won't say no."

At least she'd get a free drink. If she couldn't find a job, maybe she'd spend her time saving damsels in distress at bars. Marlis followed her to two empty stools at a high top table in the back. Nearby, a group of women held their heads close together while they murmured and glanced around nervously. A female posungi in the corner nursed a drink, her thin facial tendrils swaying in time to the music.

After the server took their order, Emmy smiled brightly at Marlis and leaned in to speak over the loud music. "Are you here for the interview, too?"

Marlis perked up. "I am looking for a job. Who's interviewing?"

"Oh," Emmy's face blanched. "You didn't get an invite? I just assumed..."

Her brief hope dashed, Marlis picked up the drink the server had just delivered and took a long, burning swallow. "That's okay. From your appearance, the job isn't likely for a Weapons Specialist, anyway."

"Wow!" An appreciative grin split the woman's face. "I've never met a Weapons Specialist!"

"What do you do?" Marlis asked, more out of politeness than anything else. She already couldn't remember this woman's name, and would probably forget all about this conversation by the time she left the cantina.

The woman's excited smile collapsed. "I trained as a therapist. But I'm looking for something else this go-round." She looked over her shoulder as if worried about being overheard. "I hear they're interviewing for all kinds of skills. I could ask them to include you."

Marlis leaned forward. Okay, so maybe she wouldn't forget this conversation that easily. "Maybe. Who would I be working for?"

Pulling out a polycom, the woman—*what was her name? Jenna?*—plopped it down on the table in front of Marlis and tapped the screen. "Here."

A video popped into motion of a charming, dark-haired

woman speaking with the biggest, most copper-skinned man Marlis'd ever imagined. "Is that a cyborg?"

"No, they call themselves denaidans. Have you heard of them?"

The underlying thrum of conversation in the cantina changed tone, and Marlis glanced toward the door. A tall beast of a man blocked the light from the outside corridor. He scoped the area, then took the arm of a tall woman next to him and moved between the tables, directly toward Marlis's table. Marlis itched in that way that usually told her trouble was brewing, but this itch was centered low in her belly and had nothing to do with her trigger finger. "Holy hotness."

Jenna or Emma or whatever her name was looked up from the video and gasped. "That's them! I recognize the woman."

Now that she mentioned it, Marlis did recognize the woman as the one from the video, but she couldn't stop looking at the man. His black beard was plaited with small silver beads, and his long hair hung down his back in banded ropes. As he scanned the cantina, his eyes locked with hers, a steely, gunmetal blue that sent tingles straight to her core.

Against her wrist, Twerp vibrated gently to inform her of her increasing heart rate.

She picked up her drink and finished it in one gulp. That guy looked like he could hold his own in a gun fight, knife fight, or any other fight she could imagine. Against her will, Marlis could imagine other things she'd like him to hold, as well.

Without taking her eyes off him, she said, "I think I'd like to apply for a job."

Chapter Four

The interior of The Junk Heap was the same as Noatak remembered—cirripi-laced air and the thrum of scattered conversations. The headache from taking the burn without shielding made his head throb in time to the wailing music, and a familiar little voice in his head said, *nothing a hit wouldn't cure.* It took all of Noatak's willpower to look away from the jittery stim vendor skulking near the entrance. He hadn't felt this much need in a very long time. *Does it matter if you lapse?*

Keeping his hand lightly on Joy's arm, he focused on their task. He might not have a future, but his crew was relying on him for theirs. Not that he believed this bar was the place to find a decent crew, let alone suitable mates.

Joy leaned close and murmured to him, "We should order drinks to fit in. You okay with that?"

His gaze flicked to the stim vendor once more. The wiry human met his gaze with the bloodshot eyes of a heavy user. Noatak swallowed and turned toward the back of the bar. Alcohol was her captain's vice, not his, but a drink sounded pretty good right now. "Sure. Whatever."

Clusters of women had gathered at the tables in the back, and Noatak's gaze came to rest on a stunning blonde. The holster on her hip made him raise an eyebrow. He'd met plenty of female soldiers during his service with the troopers, but she was by far the sexiest thing he'd ever laid eyes on. Rounded curves some might call top-heavy, yet strong in posture. Perfect alabaster skin marked only by a crooked scar on her chin.

You're not here to ogle the women, he reminded himself, turning to scan the rest of the room. Joy had hand-selected the applicants from the comments on her documentary, but that didn't mean there weren't any troopers or Syndicorp spies in the bar. Not to mention the crew of the *Hardship* had a Cartel bounty on their heads since they'd rescued Lisa from the Cartel's clutches.

Assessing the other cantina patrons, he noted a round table that hosted three scantily clad humans he guessed were sex workers, two female and one male. In the far corner slouched a mousy-type posungi female nursing a drink, her pale orange facial tendrils writhing. At the nearest table, a pair of human women sat side-by-side, spines ramrod straight, ankles crossed, and hands clasped in their laps as if they awaited an interview at a bank.

He selected a chair facing the cantina entrance, his back to the mousy woman in the corner. While Joy ordered drinks, he allowed his gaze to drift back toward the woman with the pistol, taking brief note of the small brunette sitting across from her. Both women met his eyes without hesitation. The brunette smiled lightly, nodding once in greeting. The blonde didn't smile, just took his measure. She wasn't threatening, just watchful. Cautious. Poised.

Anaq, she could probably take you in a fight. How warped was it that his groin stirred at the idea?

He turned to Joy. "Start with the blonde over there."

Joy shrugged one shoulder. "Fine by me."

Meeting the woman's tawny-eyed gaze once more, he crooked a finger to beckon her over. Her sculpted brows rose a fraction, then she whispered something to her friend and rose. Shoulders square, she strode toward him. From the sex-worker table, feminine voices complained they'd arrived first. He ignored them, watching the lithe way the woman moved. Her pale blonde hair was cut to shoulder length and gleaming.

Joy smiled brightly, gesturing toward the seat across from her. "We're glad you decided to come." She looked down at the polycom she'd pulled from her pocket. "I'm Joy, First Mate of the *PV Kinship,* and this is Noatak, First Mate of the *PV Hardship.* What's your name?"

The blonde sat. "Marlis Swan."

Frowning, Joy ran a finger over the screen. "I don't have your name on my list."

"I know." Marlis gestured toward the small brunette she'd been sitting near. "She told me about the interview. I need a job."

Instinct to use his ionic senses to measure her heart rate and breathing welled up inside Noatak. He wasn't used to making choices without it, especially about someone this intriguing.

Joy turned to him in uncertainty, but he kept his eyes forward. If he couldn't use his powers, he couldn't afford to miss a single cue, especially since he wanted to hire this woman on the spot. He leaned in slightly, nodding toward her gun. "What kind of work you looking for?"

Marlis pulled the E-11 from her hip and set it on the table, muzzle pointed away from them. "I'm trained in small arms and some hand-to-hand. Best shot in my class."

Pulling out the gun had been a bold move in the crowded bar. He liked it. She was straightforward. Honest. He slid a hand toward it. "May I?"

"Please."

He lifted the weapon. "Blackstar E-11 zero-recoil."

"Full-bore-plus with a custom trigger," Marlis added with obvious pride. "I have other models, but this one's my favorite."

"Nice." Noatak found himself nodding and handed the weapon back. "Where'd you train?"

Marlis took a deep breath and released it as if steadying for a sniper shot. "I come from a long line of troopers." She placed the gun back in its holster and lifted her chin slightly. "And before you ask why I'm not in the service,

I'll tell you. I blew up at my recruiter. Kinda ruined my chances."

The hope that had been building inside Noatak took a nose dive. Captain Qaiyaan had specifically said to weed out anyone directly in service to Syndicorp or the troopers, and here he was talking to a legacy brat. *You have to turn her away.* Not a good sign for the very first interview.

Joy tilted her head, her camera eye contracting and expanding. "Why'd you blow up at your recruiter?"

"He wanted to turn drill practice into a history lesson." Marlis wrinkled her nose. "Let's just say I'm no good at history."

Beneath the table, Noatak nudged Joy's leg. This wasn't a documentary, it was an interview, and if they expected to talk to all these women, they didn't have time to play around. Hard as it was to pass Marlis over, Noatak forced his attention to the next applicant. "Sorry, Miss Swan. I don't think we need any more hired guns right now."

The tension in the air tasted like ozone, zinging against Noatak's senses even without him engaging his ionic power.

Marlis balled her fists in her lap, then nodded once and returned to her seat near the petite brunette. Noatak realized he was watching her firm backside when Joy poked him and hissed in his ear. "Hired guns are exactly what we need."

"Too dangerous. Her family's corp."

"So? Mine is, too."

She had a valid point; her mother was one of Syndicorp's top CEOs—but that didn't erase his captain's orders. "She wasn't even on your list. We didn't and don't have time to vet her. Running interviews for the Resistance right under Syndicorp's nose is dangerous enough. Let's move on."

Joy shook her head, letting out a frustrated sigh. "I'm keeping her name for future reference."

"Do what you like." Noatak signaled to a woman with brilliant blue hair sitting at the sex-worker table. The three rose together, but Noatak shook his head. "One at a time."

The second woman giggled, but she and the male sat down, allowing their blue-haired companion to approach. She jiggled in all the right places as she walked, taking a seat across from Noatak and leaning forward so her ample breasts rested on the tabletop. "Whatever you want, baby. I know how to play nice."

Noatak crossed his arms and leaned back in his seat to escape the cloying scent of her perfume. "Name?"

After verifying the woman was on her list, Joy asked several questions, then raised an eyebrow at Noatak. To be honest, he'd only been half-listening to the interview. Marlis had put him on edge in more ways than one, and he was seriously thinking about doing business with that stim vendor near the door. He met the applicant's half-lidded gaze. "You have any skills except for the obvious?"

Hardness rose in her eyes, her lips pressing into a grim line. She crossed her arms over her cleavage. "I gotta get off this station. Just tell me what to do and I'll do it."

Damn, he wished he could just ping her and be done with this. "You willing to leave your friends over there behind?"

Her nostrils flared, and she nodded. "Anything."

"Thank you. We'll be in touch." He dismissed her.

As soon as she was out of earshot, Joy leaned over and

glared at him. "Are you discriminating against sex workers, too?"

He shook his head. "It's not her line of work I object to. She and her friends might act like they play nice together, but I suspect they'd stab each other in the back if the opportunity arose. Don't need that kind of loyalty."

Joy sighed and called the next woman over.

They continued the interviews while Noatak tried to keep his eyes off of Marlis. Unfortunately, the only other place he wanted to look was the corner where the stim vendor sat, and the growing desire within him was consuming all rational thought. He could forget everything for a little while so easily. *What are you waiting for?*

They began interviewing one of the amazingly boring bank women. Unable to take another obviously rehearsed answer, he rose. "Please excuse me a moment."

With purposeful strides, he moved toward the door, shouldering past the stim vendor and out of the confines of the cantina. If he didn't get away from temptation, he would suffocate. He closed his eyes and let his head fall back, breathing in the scent of roasted kemeg from a cart across the way.

Pull it together, Noatak. But the self-talk did little good. He was pissed. He wanted—needed—a distraction, and he needed it now.

As if in answer to his prayer, a gunshot cracked from inside the cantina, followed by screams and the distinctive zing from an E-11 pistol. He spun, realizing he'd left Joy alone. *"Uminaq!"*

The yanipa-nimayu bouncer was blocking the door, his six stocky legs planted firmly in Noatak's way. Calling up an ionic pulse, Noatak thrust him aside and stepped through the doorway, pulse pistol drawn. Between the milling bar patrons, Joy moved toward him, her face pallid. The brunette who'd been next to Marlis supported her under one arm while Marlis flanked her other side, pistol leveled toward the rear of the bar. Blood splotched Joy's light orange mechanic's shirt and coated her fingers.

"What the fuck's going on?" he asked as the trio reached him at the door. At the back of the cantina where they'd been sitting, people were shouting for medics.

"Just a scratch," Joy said through gritted teeth, her face pale and beaded with sweat.

The petite brunette helping her said, "I have some medical training. I'll get her to safety and check it out."

He nodded. "Thanks."

Marlis paused beside him, still alert for trouble at the back of the bar. "That posungi sitting behind her pulled an old-fashioned Bud-9 rimfire."

"Aiming for Joy? Or was she caught in the crossfire?"

"No idea, but I took the posungi down with a headshot." She shook her head. "I didn't think ballistic weapons were legal on a space station."

He raised an eyebrow. "They're not. The Cartel uses them, though, because they're concealable but not powerful enough to puncture hull plating."

A crowd had gathered outside the cantina doors, peering cautiously inside. Station enforcers were shouting at people to get out of the way as they tried to push through.

He glanced around. "If the attack came from the Cartel, we need to get off the station immediately. They all but own enforcement on this station."

Marlis kept pace with him all the way back to the shuttle, where she finally holstered her weapon.

"Thanks for the help," he said.

She tilted her head. "Still not in the market for a hired gun?"

"*Uminaq*," he grumbled. He owed her one, and he couldn't just leave her here to face the Cartel alone. Thrusting his pistol back into his belt, he held out a hand. "Welcome aboard the *Hardship*."

Chapter Five

Marlis wanted to run through the corridors to retrieve her gear, but she forced herself to keep to a brisk pace, trying not to draw attention to herself. After a quick idiot-check of her bunk at the hostel where she'd been staying, she hurried back to Noatak's shuttle with the reassuring weight of her rifle case against her back. She could hardly wait to call her sister to tell her the news. Who knew getting into a gunfight in a bar would be her ticket to the future? Her first ever live-fire combat had left behind an exhilaration that bordered on a drug, and Twerp hadn't stopped buzzing, but she knew her racing pulse was elation, not stress. *Let Dad try to stop me now.*

She stowed her gear and settled into a nav-grav seat next to Emmy, who'd also been offered a place on the crew. Emmy looked shell-shocked and pale, her blouse still stained with Joy's blood.

"You make a pretty good medic," Marlis said, trying to cheer her new friend up. Through the open cockpit door ahead, she could see the edge of Noatak's shoulder and muscular arm as he prepped to disengage from the station.

"Luckily, her wound doesn't appear to be life-threatening," Emmy replied, strapping in. "I didn't even see that posungi coming. I'm glad you were there."

Marlis grinned at the praise and shrugged. "Seems I excel at saving damsels in distress."

Emmy laughed and pointed toward Marlis's wrist. "You're buzzing."

Marlis sighed and looked at her wrist. "Calm down, Twerp. I'm fine."

"I feel obligated to tell you there is a fourteen point two percent risk of this endeavor leading to human trafficking," Twerp said. "I suggest removing yourself from this vessel at once."

"You have an AI!" Emmy twisted in her seat to look closer.

Trying to sound nonchalant, Marlis said. "It's just to remind me of appointments and stuff."

Twerp emitted an offended chirp. "I am a Wenzix model 15B, designed to provide space-time orientation through integrated biometric feedback."

Marlis clapped a hand over her wristband, muffling the AI's voice. She glanced toward the cockpit, relieved Noatak or Joy didn't appear to have heard. Would they change their minds if they knew about her condition? She couldn't afford to lose this job because of an AI with a big mouth.

"I worked with a client who had a 15B during my internship." Emmy raised her eyebrows. "Anger management issues."

Marlis let out a controlled breath. "Please don't mention it to anyone."

Emmy seemed to consider a moment, then nodded. "Of course. That's a cute name for an AI, by the way."

"Thank you," Twerp said brightly.

Grimacing, Marlis resisted the urge to bash her wrist against the nearest hard surface.

Emmy shifted her gaze to the cockpit, her amused expression shifting to worry. "I never considered we might be involving ourselves with slavers. They *were* only interviewing women."

Marlis looked at Noatak's broad shoulders and the way his muscles rippled beneath his thin shirt as he shifted in his seat to adjust controls. The alien practically oozed sexual tension, yet she didn't get the sense he was skeevy. Not that her hormones would give one flicker of objection if he wanted to throw her down in a wrestling match, preferably a naked one. She tended to have a good sixth sense when it came to danger. "I don't think Noatak's the type to run a sex ring." She patted her pistol against her hip. "And if he is, he'll regret it."

Outside the view screen, the pointed tip of one of the station's many communication arrays slipped past as they entered open space. Noatak's deep voice came over the comm. "Engaging burn."

The slightly nauseating thrill of the shuttle's drive rolled through her stomach. In what felt like a half a heartbeat, the cycle ended and the universe seemed to level out. *Huh, short burn.* They must not be too far from Noatak's ship. What'd he say its name was? Her sister was bound to ask.

Twerp reported. "Marlis, you'll be pleased to know your vitals have returned to acceptable levels."

"Twerp, I don't need a verbal report unless I'm in danger, okay?" Next time they stopped at a space station, she was buying a replacement earbud. She might not be able to shut the thing up, but she could restrict who heard its outbursts.

The cockpit's view screen was filled with velvety, star-studded blackness, and it took a moment for Marlis to spot the small, half-moon-shaped body of a D-class space craft blocking the pinpricks of light, its battle-scarred hull painted a dull black. A slice of light appeared in the darkness as the cargo bay doors opened. Noatak guided the shuttle slowly inside, settling to the deck with a slight thump. Behind Marlis's nav-grav seat, the shuttle's hatch hissed open with a rush of unfamiliar scents.

Noatak swiveled in his seat to look at his passengers. "Welcome aboard the *Hardship*."

Repeating the name to herself in the hope of remembering it for later, she rose and retrieved her rucksack and weapons. One strap over each shoulder, she followed Emmy down the ramp to the deck. This was about to be her new home. Her new purpose. How many people were on the crew? She was going to have to remember names. Protocols. Who knew what else? She focused on her breathing, keeping her pulse under control. The last thing she needed was Twerp piping up right now.

Compared to the vastness of the carrier she'd grown up on, the ship's tiny cargo bay felt almost cozy. The shuttle took up most of the space, butting up against a set of stairs connected to a grated catwalk overhead. A ginger-haired man with copper skin like Noatak's pounded down the catwalk at a run, slammed both hands on the rail, and in one swift move launched up and over the edge. Marlis didn't even have time to register shock before he landed gracefully on the deck in front of her.

"Hi! I'm Tovik!" He thrust an oil-stained hand toward Emmy, teeth gleaming in a self-satisfied grin.

Marlis blinked as the scent of flowery perfume wafted over her and stared at his bare feet. With that entrance, she wasn't likely to forget his name any time soon. He was younger than Noatak, but just as tall in a gangly fashion that promised more muscles to come.

Emmy smiled warmly and set her suitcase down to shake his hand. "Emmy Quick."

He turned to Marlis, and she accepted his handshake. "Marlis Swan."

"Wow. This is exciting." He continued pumping her hand and nodding, looking from Emmy to her as if he'd never before seen a human. Then he did a double-take at something behind her and dropped her hand. "What happened?"

Marlis turned to find Noatak descending the ramp, one arm around Joy's waist. Guilt flickered in Marlis's throat. A good crew member would've remembered to help.

Tovik surged forward and took up Joy's opposite side, sliding an arm around her. "*Anaq*! Joy! Are you all right?"

Joy smiled wanly. "I'll be fine as soon as Mek gives me some painkillers."

Tovik's brows drew together as he shifted his gaze to Noatak. "Kashatok's gonna kill you."

Noatak scowled right back at him. "She said she's fine, Tovik." His nose wrinkled. "Are you wearing perfume?"

The younger man's copper face flushed blue green, his gaze flitting to where Emmy and Marlis stood. "I heard ladies like flowers."

"Don't make me laugh, it hurts," Joy wheezed, her arms clutching her injured torso. "I think you've been getting some bad advice, my friend."

A third copper-skinned man arrived from the stairs, his clean-shaven face austere in comparison to Noatak and Tovik's well-groomed beards. He strode forward with a med scanner, completely intent on Joy until he saw Emmy's blouse. "You hurt, too?"

Emmy shook her head, seemingly at a loss for words as she craned her neck to look up at his face.

"Don't be rude, Mek." Tovik frowned. He turned to look at Emmy and Marlis. "This is Mek, our ship's doctor. He's not usually such a *terpak*."

Noatak released Joy into Mek's care. "You got this?"

Mek nodded, slipping an arm around the injured woman. He smiled tightly as he passed Marlis and Emmy on his way toward the stairs. "Sorry to be so abrupt. I look forward to talking to you later."

"Tovik." Noatak picked up the suitcase Emmy had set down and thrust it toward the younger man. "Drop their bags in the bunk room, then join us in the galley."

"Aye-aye." Tovik took Emmy's suitcase and held out a hand for Marlis's rucksack.

Marlis clutched her shoulder strap tighter. She didn't like to let other people handle her weapons. "I can carry my own bags."

"Suit yourself." Without preamble, Tovik bunched his legs and leaped into the air—if it could be called leaping. The move was more like a short flight, leaving the scent of perfume in his wake. He landed lightly on the catwalk above and turned to glance over his shoulder with a self-satisfied grin. "See you soon."

"Show off," Noatak muttered before leading them toward the stairs.

Marlis followed him up the steps, her boots ringing on the metal grates. "Are all of you so… nimble?"

"No." Noatak spoke without turning around, voice cold. "Don't let him fool you into thinking he has superpowers. Our species—most of our species—have the ability to manipulate ionically-charged molecules in immediate proximity to us."

Marlis had never been good at school, and his vocabulary took some pondering for her to unravel. While she did, Emmy pulled ahead of her to walk next to Noatak as they reached the catwalk. "Like telekinesis? That's fascinating!"

Telekinesis. That word she knew. How was she going to keep up with a crew that could move shit with their brains? Maybe Noatak'd been serious when he'd said they didn't need more hired guns.

They reached the hatch and stepped through into a narrow corridor. Noatak led them past several doors into a galley where a large oval table surrounded by chairs took up most of the space. He gestured to the seats. "Now that you're on board, we need to lay down some ground rules."

Marlis set her bags next to the nearest chair and sat, glancing around at the closed cabinets lining the walls. She wasn't familiar with the layout of D-class ships, but if this tiny galley served the entire crew, no wonder Noatak was extra picky about who he hired. Crew members had to get along. A flare of pride glowed in her chest; she'd made the cut.

Emmy took the seat to her left, hands clasped nervously in her lap as she watched Noatak move to the other end of the table. Marlis pulled out her polycom to take notes. Twerp recorded everything for her to review later if she wanted, but her therapist encouraged her to write things down for herself. She had to stay focused if she expected to prove to her new crew she belonged here.

"You'll both serve here on the *Hardship* until Captain Qaiyaan gets back." Noatak powered up a wall screen between the cabinets, bringing up the ship's data screen. "He and Kashatok may rearrange your assignments later, though."

While Marlis was jotting the names, the young denaidan who'd taken Emmy's bag burst in, chest heaving and eyes glittering. He yanked out the seat next to Marlis, looking over her shoulder at her polycom. She twisted her head to glare up at him. She hated it when people read over her shoulder. Her notes were none of his business.

Pausing with his backside half-lowered onto the chair, his smile faltered. Still, the kid was incorrigible, and winked before pushing the chair back in and moved down several seats.

Marlis swallowed, feeling a little guilty. She'd already forgotten the young man's name, and when she glanced back at her notes, she'd also forgotten who Kashatok was. *Dammit.* She'd written it down, so it was important. She needed repetition. Lots and lots of repetition. "Who's Kashatok again?"

"Captain of the *Kinship*." Noatak pointed to a K-class freighter on the screen. "Joy's his First Mate."

"And his mate-mate!" The young man chimed in, green eyes dancing.

"Enough, Tovik." Noatak glowered at him.

Tovik, Marlis repeated to herself, staring hard at him to ingrain his face in her mind.

The young man beamed under her scrutiny and Marlis felt herself flushing. *Fuck.* She was going to give this guy the wrong idea if she wasn't careful. She lowered her gaze to her polycom and put his name there with the words *don't shoot the puppy*. When she shifted her attention back to Noatak, he'd started a video rolling.

"You two have the honor of being among the first recruits for the Resistance. Our fleet is comprised..."

She wrote *Resistance* onto the polycom. Had they mentioned a resistance during the interview? She could ask Twerp about it later. For now, she had to assume that since she was here, she must've been okay with it. *Pay attention, Marlis.*

"I know the odds are against us, and the corporation is powerful. But more and more of their lies—"

Marlis was getting the feeling that this crew wasn't conducting the kind of legitimate business her sister'd had in mind. What had she gotten herself into? Throat tight, she raised a hand. "Are you talking about Syndicorp?"

Wariness flashed through Noatak's eyes. "Yes."

Emmy spoke up. "I was going to show her the video back in the cantina, but then the fight broke out. Maybe she could watch it now?"

Noatak's jaw worked as if he wanted to say no, but Tovik jumped up. "She hasn't seen it?" He tapped the screen on the wall. "Joy did a great job putting all the facts together."

A RealTime News logo appeared, followed by Joy's face.

Marlis forced herself to focus on the screen. She refused to believe her dad had been right about her getting into trouble. *Get all the facts, then decide.* That's what her therapist always urged her to do before she let her emotions get the best of her. Breathing in through her nose and out through her mouth, she settled back to watch.

Joy described a planet called Denaida-daru, where Syndicorp had been testing a genetically altered virus. Marlis'd never paid much attention to technology that didn't relate to weapons, and a lot of what Joy said didn't mean anything to her. She gathered that somehow the virus had mutated and created a cancer that killed off all the women and most of the men on the planet.

The emerald-green planet on the screen developed white spots, each spot widening and growing until the entire planet glowed like a small sun. "Rather than continue to work on a cure or make amends to the surviving population, Syndicorp sterilized the planet."

Marlis gasped out loud. She'd never heard of a populated planet being sterilized.

"You may be asking why you've never heard of Denaida-daru, also called K-4H10," Joy continued. "Because there would be backlash against the heinous act, Syndicorp started a war to divert attention. Remember Pulati?" The video cut to an all-too-familiar scene on what had been a lovely, tree-lined plaza. A plaza littered with bodies and blood and debris.

The floor beneath Marlis's chair seemed to wobble as she stared at the footage. Cut scenes from the war itself filled the room, making the walls close in around her. She heard her mother's scream cut off.

"... Not only did the people of Denaida-daru suffer genocide at corporate hands, but tens of thousands of Pulati colonists died fighting terrorists. Terrorists who were funded by Syndicorp."

While the voice on the screen kept talking, Marlis was no longer in the galley of a D-class ship. She was a ten-year-old girl lying beneath her mother's contorted body. Unable to breathe. Not daring to move. Gunfire sliced the air and trooper boots thundered against the earth.

Adrenaline surged through her veins. She couldn't breathe past the stench of blood or hear over the screams echoing in her ears. Flies tickled over her skin. Her wrist ached, and she had no idea why.

"Marlis, lower your head to your knees," a feminine voice floated through the chaos.

Marlis forced herself to focus, expecting to be staring into the muzzle of a trooper's rifle. Sure a hole would blossom in her head at any moment. *I need a gun.* She reached for her hip.

A strong hand encircled hers, gripping her fingers tightly. Keeping her from moving. Panic once again made her vision swim.

A woman's round face took shape in front of her, brown eyes concerned. "Marlis, it's just me. Emmy. It's all right."

I should know this person.

A disembodied voice chanted, "There is no danger."

The only important word in that phrase was 'danger.' Lurking danger. Marlis twisted against the grip still clamped on her hand and found herself looking into gunmetal blue eyes. Dark brows on copper skin. A beard decorated with metal beads.

Noatak's lips moved. "Cool your jets, soldier. You're safe here."

For some reason, those words cut through her fog. His hand on hers was like a lifeline. She took a deep breath. "Safe."

Cautiously and still maintaining direct eye contact, he said, "Everyone out."

The round-faced woman and another copper-skinned man with ginger hair backed out of the room. Noatak relaxed his grip on her hand, but to her relief, he didn't let go. He settled into the seat facing her. "Now tell me what this is all about."

How many therapists had asked her that? She felt like a robot as she answered, "I was in that battle."

His eyes narrowed. "You were a child when Pulati broke out."

"Yes, sir." For some reason, calling him sir made her feel

calm. Like she was a soldier instead of a victim. "I was ten."

He raised a brow and slowly withdrew his hand. "You're from the colony? I thought you said you were legacy. Your family is with the troopers."

She let out a shaky breath. Her mind had started to clear a bit. "My mother and I went to Pulati on leave. The same day as the first terrorist outbreak."

Staring numbly at the screen, Marlis recalled her earliest memories; the ones that still, no matter how hard she squelched them, haunted her nightmares. *Troopers with guns. Trooper boots marching through the plaza full of bodies. A trooper looking down the barrel of her gun straight into Marlis's eyes.* No one had ever believed her before. Now she knew her memories were true.

The terrorist attack had been orchestrated by Syndicorp.

She turned to Noatak, his name like a pinprick of sanity in her chaotic mind. "Troopers killed my mother."

Chapter Six

Noatak swallowed against the unfamiliar feelings welling inside him as Marlis described her hours on Pulati. How she'd faced down a young trooper who apparently hadn't had the stomach to finish the job and left Marlis half-dead beneath her mother's corpse. How she'd been in and out of consciousness for an entire day and into the night before rescuers arrived. How the media had put her on display as a victim without ever letting her speak.

"My first therapist said I misremembered the attack." Marlis's eyes were glassy, the scar on her chin a pale slash against her already pale skin. "Said my dad would lose his job if I told anyone and he'd be labeled a traitor. She blamed it on the damage to my brain, so I believed her. I changed my story. Troopers would never hurt innocents, right?"

She met his eyes, and he felt as if he'd just been sucked into a whirlpool. On instinct, he opened his ionic power, letting the feel of her heartbeat reach him, the subtle rhythm of her breathing. Sweet, feminine warmth and the subtle scent of musk from her skin caused a sense of protectiveness he'd never experienced before.

Uminaq, this wasn't the time or the place for softness. He was still trying to make up his mind about keeping her on board. His gut told him she was genuine, but his ever-doubtful logic insisted this had to be a complicated ruse. Why else would a legacy trooper end up in that cantina at that exact time?

As he worked to get himself under control, Marlis rose, hands clenched into fists at her sides. The wrist band he'd noticed earlier was emitting a low-frequency vibration. "They made me lie to myself." Her voice held outrage. Fury. Disgust. "I thought by joining the troopers I'd be protecting people."

"Most people think that." He watched her pace the length of the table. His admiration for her strength grew with every word she spoke. "I know I did."

She turned and stared at him. "You were a trooper?"

He nodded, leaning back in his chair. He wasn't proud of his trooper days, but he found himself wanting to tell her everything. "Joined up the moment I was old enough. Good pay, worthy cause, exciting adventures. All the stuff the recruiter was selling."

"Where'd you serve?"

"SNV Riley Blue, Galactic Ops."

Her eyes grew round, and she returned unsteadily to her chair, knees brushing his as she faced him. "What I wouldn't have given to join Galactic Ops."

His thigh muscles tightened with awareness of her closeness, like a proximity alarm racing through his bloodstream. He had to focus. "Not all it's cracked up to be, believe me."

The admiration in her eyes turned to distrust.

Once more, he found himself volunteering more information than he usually felt comfortable giving. "Almost all the denaidans still alive today were in the service. Joining up was one of the few ways to get off-world. The corp didn't know much about our physiology and while they studied my ionic abilities, they had me on almost constant recovery stims. After I went AWOL, I nearly killed myself getting off the stuff."

"You went AWOL?" Her tawny eyes widened.

He let out a sardonic laugh. Of course she'd care more about him going AWOL than she would about stim addiction. "Had to get away before Syndicorp could silence us." His nostrils flared as he recalled how many of his trooper *iluq* had come to mysterious ends immediately following his planet's Termination.

"Silence you for what?"

"They destroyed my home world, remember?" He frowned. Apparently, she'd been so engrossed in her own horrible memories she'd forgotten.

"Oh, yeah." The rosy flush on her cheeks was unaccountably appealing. She blinked several times, then put one hand over her forehead, gaze darting around the galley. "I need to call my sister."

That surprised him. Why this sudden urge for family? He crossed his arms. "Absolutely not."

Scowling, Marlis dropped her hand and leaned forward to look into his eyes, her heaving breath brushing his bare forearms. "She's a trooper. So are my dad and my brother. If I join your rebellion, what do you think might happen to them? I need to warn them."

He ran his tongue over his teeth. She had a point. Did this mean she was no longer a risk? Venturing another ionic pulse to test her sincerity, he asked, "You want to join us?"

She nodded, her jaw set. "Definitely."

He could tell by the steady beat of her heart that she meant it. But he needed her to fully understand what she was getting into. "You should also know that we're wanted for piracy."

Her delicate brows drew together. "As in, raping and pillaging?"

"Not exactly, although there were a few denaidans who went that far. The bulk of us just wanted revenge against the corp. Technically, I'd call us privateers."

She narrowed an eye. "Privateers, pirates, what's the difference?"

A feminine voice erupted from her wrist band. "Pirates attack anyone. Privateers only attack enemy ships."

She clapped her hand over her wrist. "Shut up, Twerp."

He'd been aware of the buzzing at her wrist off and on since meeting her, but this was the first time he gave it any serious regard. Now suspicion blossomed inside him again. "Is that a Syndicorp AI?"

"You may call me Twerp," the muffled voice said. "I am a Wen—"

"Shut up, Twerp!" Marlis lifted her hand and banged the wristband against the table.

The AI emitted an indignant chirp but did not resume speaking.

How could he have let himself be so careless? She'd brought a Syndicorp AI on board the ship. "Who does it report to?"

She blinked, as if unsure what he was asking. "Just me."

Twerp spoke up again, its chirpy voice a cheery contrast to Marlis's. "I have successfully connected to this ship's communication array. Would you like me to send a message to your sister?"

"Dammit! Not now, Twerp." The flush he'd appreciated earlier returned to Marlis's face. She unstrapped the thing from her wrist and offered it to Noatak. "Suppose I may as well tell you now. I have trouble remembering things and I get… frustrated… easily. Twerp keeps me in line."

"I don't give an *anaq* about all that." Noatak grabbed the band. "Tell it to disconnect immediately."

She stiffened, and he wondered for a moment if she was going to protest. Then she said, "Twerp, suspend all wireless connections, please."

The AI said, "If I am not connected to the ship, I will be unable to provide spatial data."

Marlis leaned forward to speak directly toward the device. "That's an order, Twerp."

"Disconnecting now. Please be careful when moving about to make note of your location."

Noatak gripped the wristband tighter. He wanted to smash the thing to smithereens, just to be safe. But Marlis'd complied with his request to disconnect. And she'd said something about a brain injury. "Can you get along without it?"

"I've had it since I was thirteen." Her pretty throat flexed around a swallow, and her lips were a pale line.

He rubbed his forehead. *Stop thinking of her as a woman and treat her like a soldier.* Even good soldiers sometimes needed assistance. She'd trusted in the corp, just like the rest of them, and her betrayal was real. That much he knew. But he didn't know about her AI. "I need to have it checked out before I can give it back to you."

She nodded and licked her lips. "What about contacting my sister?"

Could he blame her for wanting to be sure her family was safe? He'd do exactly the same thing. "I don't want to censor you, but we need to be careful about information leaks. What would you tell her?"

A furrow appeared between Marlis's eyebrows. "Fuck, she wouldn't believe me, anyway. I just don't want her to be caught unaware or punished because of my choices."

He reached out and put a hand on her shoulder. "Didn't you say your father and brother were also with the service?"

She looked stricken. "You think I might be a liability to this cause. That they'd be used as leverage against me."

He squeezed her shoulder lightly, unable to stop himself from imagining what her skin might feel like beneath his palm. *Ellam Cua, this woman is as addictive as stims.* He forced himself to release his grip. "We all have things that make us a liability." *Like my failing ionic heart.* "We just need to come up with something to tell them that won't connect you to the Resistance."

She drummed the fingertips of one hand on the table. "They're probably already wondering what happened to me."

"We'll work on a story together." He held up the AI's wrist band. "I'll get this back to you as soon as I can. Meanwhile, consider yourself on probation."

"Thank you for giving me a chance to prove myself." She rose and held out her hand. "You don't know how much that means to me."

He took her handshake, marveling at the fine bone structure engulfed by his grip. The perfect woman dropped in his lap when he was least able to make her his. He could picture *Ellam Cua,* their trickster god, laughing at him right now. He released her sharply, trying to reign in his stupid feelings, and grabbed her duffel bag. "I'll show you to your bunk."

She picked up her weapons case and followed him down the corridor to the women's bunk room where Emmy was waiting.

He left her there and headed for engineering to find Tovik. The young denaidan wasn't there, so he went to the med bay; if the kid wasn't in engineering, he'd be with Joy. Too bad that scoundrel, Kashatok, had claimed her heart, or the kid might've had his first taste of love.

As Noatak rounded the corner toward the med bay, he heard them discussing flux modulators. The two sat cross-legged on the single bed facing each other, Joy's legs covered by a sheet and her upper half in a medical gown. The screen behind her displayed her vitals in various colors.

Noatak frowned. "Aren't you supposed to be resting?"

"I can't, not when Kashatok's not here." She smiled sadly. Joy wasn't what he'd call pretty, but when she smiled, he could see why Kashatok had been attracted to her.

"Maybe you and Tovik can tackle this together." He held out the wrist band.

"What is it?" Tovik reached for it.

The AI's voice rose from the band. "Please return me to Marlis immediately."

Tovik raised his brows. "An AI?"

"My name is Twerp. I request your assistance returning me to my rightful owner."

Joy shifted her attention to Noatak, brows furrowed. "I heard she had a breakdown. Is she okay?"

Twerp chimed in, "I must have physical contact with my owner to provide biometric feedback and guidance."

Joy glanced from the AI to Noatak. "Um, thank you, Twerp. But I was asking Noatak."

Noatak shook his head. He'd never met a sentient machine, and he wasn't sure he liked it. "Marlis is fine. Turns out she has her own reasons for wanting to get back at Syndicorp. You want to know more, you can ask her." He pointed at the AI in Tovik's hand. "Can you make sure that thing's not bugged before I give it back to her?"

"I'll get on it right now." Tovik pocketed the device and stood up. "See you later, Joy."

She smiled at him. "Bye, Tovik. Let me know if you need any help."

The kid padded out of the room, his bare feet silent on the deck. Noatak remained, feeling uncomfortable as he looked at the monitor behind Joy's bed. He should say something, but apologizing wasn't his usual style.

"Don't worry, I'm fine." Joy stretched her legs beneath

the sheets and leaned back against the pillow, closing her eyes. "It's not your fault, you know."

Given an opening, Noatak sat on the stool nearby. "I shouldn't have left you alone."

"I should've paid more attention." She shook her head. "I thought the Cartel would only be targeting Lisa. In hindsight, Whylon Station probably wasn't the best choice for a meeting."

Just then, Mek came around the corner into the med bay. "I just passed Tovik in the hall. He said Marlis has an AI. Is it a medical unit?"

"You'll have to ask her. She mentioned having a previous brain injury."

"Interesting. I'd like to check her out." Mek looked toward the door as if intending to call her in this very moment.

Noatak's throat felt suddenly dry as he imagined the doctor examining Marlis. Would he ask her to undress? He'd never before considered that Mek had an unfair advantage. *Stop being possessive about something you can't have.* He forced himself to shrug and kept his gaze on Joy. "You're the doc."

"Should we keep her on the crew?" Joy asked.

"She'll make an excellent crewman," Noatak snapped back before Mek could respond. "And she saved your ass. I could use someone like her at my back."

Joy chortled. "I think Noatak may have a crush on our new Weapons Specialist."

He glared at her. "Appreciating a skilled gunman is its own thing."

She scrunched her eyes in a snotty little sister kind of smile. "Uh, huh."

"Marlis's brain damage would be an interesting study." Mek tapped his forefinger against his chin. "I wonder if the nanites would repair her?"

The microscopic nano-computers were designed to alter brain structure and create something called cyber-sensitivity in humans—the ability to access computer systems remotely without any additional hardware. They were also the only thing that allowed the denaidans to have mates. Noatak didn't know whether to be excited Marlis might be the next candidate for the nanites or pissed. If she began the process now, someone else could end up bonding with her before his heart was fixed. "We only have one sample left, right? Maybe you should use it on a more steady patient."

"The sample's degrading quickly," Mek answered. "We need to inoculate a new host as soon as possible. And in Marlis's case, the nanites will serve a dual purpose."

"You still can't get my samples to survive?" Joy asked.

"No matter what I do, when I separate them from your dendritic tissue, it corrupts their operating system. They become completely inert." Unlike Lisa's nanites, which had died off completely during her mating with Qaiyaan, Joy's nanites had fused to her nervous system when she'd joined with Kashatok.

"We should at least wait to decide until Qaiyaan and the others get back," Noatak said. "Let her meet the rest of the crew before she commits to something as serious as the nanites."

Mek shrugged. "The longer we wait, the less viable the sample becomes."

"If they come back with Doug, we'll have all the samples we need," Noatak argued.

"And if they come back with nothing?"

The captains had gone to meet a black-market contact for information about the secret Syndicorp lab where Lisa's brother, Doug—the original nanite test subject— was being kept. But they'd come back from previous meetings empty-handed. Mek's sample might be their only hope for mates.

Pacing the short distance to the door and back, Noatak balled his hands into fists at his sides. He wasn't ready for things to be moving so fast. "We don't even know if the nanites will help her. They nearly killed Lisa." He spun and thrust a finger in Joy's direction. "And she'd be blind now if it wasn't for the camera implant."

"Calm down, *iluq*." Mek made a calming motion with both hands. "We let the nanites grow too close to critical saturation in previous instances. Next time, I plan to keep the host under constant supervision."

The host. It sounded so cold. So clinical. When they'd first come up with the plan to hire women and inoculate them, it'd been tactical. A means to an end. Now that they were talking about Marlis, it had become personal. "This isn't a Syndicorp test lab. You're talking about a person."

"Guys." Joy tilted her head. "We haven't even asked her yet. She could say no. Don't get so riled up."

Mek pursed his lips and gave Noatak a meaningful look. "I think she's the best candidate right now, regardless of any extenuating circumstances."

"*Anaq.*" Noatak blew out a breath and looked at a spot on the wall near Joy's monitor. "Fine."

They needed a host. He couldn't deny it. The future of his entire race depended on it.

And unless Mek came up with a solution for his heart, Marlis would end up pairing with someone else.

Marlis had grown up sharing a room with her sister, but the accommodations on the *Hardship* were a little ridiculous—barely more than a walkway between two sets of bunk beds. Inside the lower bunk compartment on the right, Emmy'd hung a picture of herself with a golden retriever. A menagerie of tiny stuffed animals dotted her pillow, and several articles of clothing lay scattered over the blanket in the process of being folded.

Tossing her rucksack onto the bunk above Emmy's, Marlis asked, "Do we have roommates?"

"I think we're the only ones in here so far."

Fewer names to remember would be good. She examined the compartment that would be her bunk. Two inset shelves took up the entire wall inside, yet seemed hardly adequate for her clothing, let alone any other gear. "Where can I stow my weapons?"

Emmy cocked her head. "They probably have a weapons locker to store guns."

"I like to keep my weapons at hand." Marlis thrust her rifle case across the mattress.

Rising from the bottom bunk, Emmy's head barely cleared the top edge of the mattress. "Are you going to try to fit everything in here?"

"I keep my E-11 beneath my pillow. Maybe I can install a mounting bracket at the foot to hold Fanny." Marlis stroked her MCS6 rifle.

"So..." Emmy cleared her throat. "Exactly how many gun fights have you been in?"

Marlis flushed. "That was my first, actually."

Emmy widened her eyes. "Wow. You reacted so fast, I assumed you did that sort of thing all the time."

"Thank you." Marlis's reflexes were the one thing her brain damage never seemed to adversely affect and the only good thing the recruitment trainer'd ever said about her.

"Do you think you killed Joy's attacker?"

A vague recollection of a pulse blast leaving her gun in slow motion and connecting squarely with the posungi's forehead intruded on her thoughts. Marlis's throat felt unaccountably thick all of a sudden. Until the cantina, she'd only engaged in mock exercises, shooting at digital targets. *Damn memory. Only comes back at the worst times.* She swallowed and answered, "I... I guess so."

"Is that why you were upset in the galley?" Emmy put a gentle hand on her forearm.

"Not exactly." She'd just told Noatak everything, and for the second time today she realized how odd it felt to be talking to people who didn't already know what she'd been through. People who didn't automatically categorize her as unfixable. If she and Emmy were going to be co-workers, bunk-mates, hopefully even friends, Marlis might as well tell her everything, just like she had with Noatak. "We're all in the Resistance together, so I guess it's only fair you know."

"Okay." Emmy swept some scattered lingerie aside and sat on her bunk, looking up expectantly.

Wishing for Twerp's reassuring buzz, Marlis thought, *There is no danger.* She sat on the bunk and leaned back against the footboard, pulling one knee up. As she related her time on Pulati, new memories cropped up, bits and pieces of detail she'd never dared voice. "My therapist kept asking if I was angry with my mother for failing to protect me. But all I recall is being happy Mom wouldn't be on duty, so I'd have her all to myself."

Her voice cracked. Every inch of her body trembled and her hand itched for the comforting grip of her E-11.

Emmy reached behind her and pulled a stuffed unicorn from her pillow, dropping it onto Marlis's lap. "Here."

Marlis stared at the plush toy, then back at Emmy. Did Emmy think Marlis was being a baby? "What's this for?"

"I just noticed you were clenching and unclenching your hands. Sometimes having something to hold on to helps when you're talking about stressful stuff. If you don't want it, that's okay."

"Why did you even bring these?"

"I'm sentimental, I guess, and I had room. They remind me of happier days."

The plush toy did remind Marlis of how innocent she'd been before the trauma. Of a childhood that had been cut off too soon. Her breath shuddered as early memories crowded her thoughts. "Mom was trying really hard not to be a soldier so we could have fun." Marlis felt a wistful smile tug the corner of her mouth. "She said someone else could police the universe for a few days and even joked with some of the troopers the morning before it all happened." She looked up into Emmy's eyes. "The same troopers who then shot her at point blank range and left me to die."

Emmy gasped, eyes glistening with tears. "That's awful."

Marlis dug her fingers into the unicorn's soft curves, wanting to rip it in half. "How could I forget that?"

"We're told to trust troopers from the moment we can walk. And Syndicorp wanted you to forget. You'd probably be dead right now if you'd remembered."

"You think these pirates can really mount a resistance? That there's any hope of making Syndicorp pay for what they did?"

"I certainly hope so." Emmy frowned. "Although I'm not sure exactly how I'm going to be able to help."

"You did a great job patching up Joy." The change in focus felt good, like the ship's gravity had just lessened. "Maybe you can help the doctor?"

"I had to do a medical rotation for my psychiatric internship, but blood makes me woozy." Emmy shuddered theatrically.

Marlis raised her brows. "Really? I never would've guessed. You did great."

A knock at the doorframe drew their attention, and Noatak leaned into the room. "Settled in?"

"I think so." Emmy smiled at him and pointed to the bunk above their heads. "Although Marlis really could use some space for her extra guns."

"I don't have *extra* guns." Marlis glanced at the unicorn in her lap and quickly thrust it back toward Emmy. "And Emmy's not going to have anywhere to sleep with all these stuffed animals."

Noatak's gaze flickered over the unicorn before pausing on something near Marlis's knee. A twitch of a smile lifted the corner of his mouth. She followed the direction of his gaze to a lacy orange pair of panties—definitely not trooper issue—but even though they weren't hers, she flushed.

"You can each have a locker in the cargo bay for extra items." His smile faded, and he stepped back into the hallway. "Marlis, do you have a few minutes? The doc would like a word with you."

"The doctor? Why?" Did this have something to do with

her breakdown in the galley? Damn it all if she'd disqualified herself from yet another job.

Noatak rubbed his temple. "He saw your AI. Wants to talk to you about it."

Twerp. Even when she wasn't wearing it, the AI was a source of trouble. Swallowing, she nodded and slid out of the bunk. Shooting a worried smile at Emmy, Marlis followed Noatak down the corridor to a small med bay.

The doctor sat on a stool inside, his back to the door as he scrolled through computer files. He must've heard their approach because he swiveled to greet them. "Marlis. I'm so glad you're here." He patted the exam table. "Please, sit."

She perched on the foot of the bed, facing the doctor. She'd been through so many physical exams, it almost felt like home again. Except that Noatak remained stiffly just inside the door. Was he worried about her? Although he'd basically said she was on probation, he seemed to want her on the crew. Hopefully, he was sticking around as an advocate, especially since she couldn't for the life of her remember the doctor's name.

"Are you familiar with nano-bots?" the doctor asked.

"Sure," she answered with a shrug. "Itty-bitty computers, right?"

"Has anyone mentioned that humans and denaidans cannot engage in sex?"

"Uh, okay. Good thing that's not what I'm here for." She found her gaze sliding toward Noatak near the door. She had no idea where this conversation could be going. Was her brain damage getting worse? She reached for her wrist, seeking Twerp's comforting presence. *Gone.* "I thought you wanted to talk to me about my AI."

Noatak made a grumbling noise and took a small step into the room. "Mek's doctoring ability is far better than his conversational skills. He's trying to say he thinks he can fix your brain damage with nanites."

"The same technology that makes a human a compatible mate for our kind," Mek added, as if that was the most important part of this conversation.

She gaped at the doctor, Twerp's warning about sex trafficking coming back to mind. "You want to mate with me?"

Mek raised both palms. "No! I mean, not me, personally. I mean—"

Noatak cut in, his huge frame somehow a threat and a comfort at the same time. "No one would dare touch you without your permission."

"Of course not!" The doctor blew out a breath. "Sexual compatibility would simply be a side effect in this instance. Our primary objective is to restore full capacity to your central nervous system."

She straightened. "You're saying the nanites can actually heal me? Restore my ability to remember stuff?"

The doctor answered, "I can't make any promises, but yes, the nanites might restore cognitive function lost due to brain damage."

"Let's do it!" She looked at the two men expectantly. "What do I need to do? Sign a waiver? What?"

The doc held up a hand. "Not so fast. I'll need to get a baseline scan first. Plus, I want you to be fully informed before we proceed. We have some requirements of you during the process."

The prospect of being healed—being normal—was making her giddy. "Whatever it takes. Let's get on with it."

"First of all, you must promise *not* to have sex while you're under treatment."

Her gaze slid inadvertently toward Noatak. "But I thought you said the nanites would make me compatible?"

The intensity that met her in Noatak's eyes felt like a tractor beam. She recognized that hunger, but never before had it caused heat to pool between her legs as it did now. Dragging her attention away, she attempted to focus on what Mek was saying.

"The nanites will change your brain structure and chemistry, making you a viable mate for denaidans, but the culmination of the sex act itself will destroy the nanites," Mek said. "This offer isn't completely altruistic—you'll be a host to grow the nanites and provide us additional inoculations, and for that, we need time."

"Oh." This was getting confusing. She needed Twerp more than ever. "When can I have my AI back? She interprets this kind of stuff for me."

"Tovik's almost finished with his check and then we'll return it," Mek said. "We want to be completely transparent about what you can expect. Rest assured that I'll monitor you closely for any adverse reactions."

"Adverse reactions? You mean side effects?" This was starting to sound less and less like a sure thing.

"You could call them that. The nanites were developed as an experiment in cyber-sensitivity. You'll likely become hyper-aware of the computer systems around you and may experience blackouts, but I believe with proper monitoring I can minimize those events."

Now Marlis was getting really confused. "I thought you said these nanites had something to do with denaidan mating. Now you're saying they were developed for something else. Where did this technology come from in the first place?"

The two men exchanged an uncomfortable glance and Noatak answered, "We got it from a secret Syndicorp lab experiment."

That didn't surprise her. Marlis rubbed her temples. The temptation to just say fuck it and agree was strong within her. She wanted to be healed. To be normal. But with this much information, she didn't trust herself to make a sound decision.

"You don't need to give us your answer now," Noatak said, shooting the doctor a glance.

Mek nodded slowly. "Correct, although sooner is better. My remaining inoculation is degrading quickly and will soon be useless unless we can find a new host." He pulled the med bay scanner from the wall toward the exam table. "Marlis, if you don't mind, I'd like to begin non-invasive baseline scans right away. That way, if you decide to proceed, we can inoculate you without delay."

"Isn't there one more thing you need to tell her?" Noatak asked in a monotone.

"Oh, right." A greenish flush crept over the doctor's face. "I get ahead of myself. We need to walk a fine line between allowing the nanites to finish the job without letting them take over your system entirely. They will need to be terminated before they reach critical saturation."

"Critical saturation? That sounds… bad." She swallowed, casting a glance toward Noatak once more. It felt as if heat waves radiated off of him, his gaze once more pulling at her like a tractor beam.

Although he was focused on her, Noatak's words were for Mek. "Could you be more obscure, doctor?"

"I'm trying not to be crude, Noatak." Mek crossed his arms.

This time, Noatak did speak directly to her. "The only way we currently have to terminate the nanite replication is with sex."

To her surprise, relief flooded her. "Oh, is that all?"

CHAPTER EIGHT

Noatak rolled over in his bunk, unable to force sleep to come. *She was going to accept the nanites.* He knew it, could sense it in her eyes and confirmed it with an ionic pulse, despite Mek's knowing glare. Noatak couldn't help it. The instinct was just too strong. What he'd discovered was that Marlis wasn't afraid, not even of the idea of mating. She was the perfect candidate. When the *Kinship* returned, the crew would be falling over themselves to court her, and he didn't think he could bear watching her accept the advances of another man.

A knock pulled him from his half-doze and his heart leaped. *Marlis?* "Come in."

Mek stepped inside, closing the door behind him. "Just what do you think you're doing?"

"Trying to sleep," Noatak grumbled, pushing down disappointment. "How's Marlis?"

"I'm not here to talk about her." Mek pointed a finger at Noatak. "I felt you ping her in there."

Throwing back the blanket, Noatak rose to grab his pants. "Asking a denaidan not to use his powers is like asking a *qilzri* bird not to fly. Spreading my wings is a reflex."

"You can't be with her." Mek crossed his arms. "I'm sorry. I know you like her, but you can't."

Noatak fastened his pants and leveled his gaze at the doctor. "It's possible I could survive mating, you know."

Mek sighed. "Or you could leave her a heartbroken widow. I know you don't want to hear it, but it's my job to remind you of the consequences."

He glared at the doctor. "*Ellam Cua*, I know the consequences. Now go back to your lab and find a way to fix me." Half a heartbeat later, he added, "Please."

"You're one stubborn *terpak*." Mek threw up his hands and turned to the door. "I'll see what I can do."

Alone in his cabin once more, Noatak knew sleep was impossible. He'd spent many sleepless night cycles wearing himself out on the punching bag in the cargo bay, trying to forget his craving for stims. Maybe it'd get his mind off Marlis, too.

Not bothering with a shirt, he entered the dimly lit corridor, the ship nearly silent during the sleep cycle. Even the hum of the engines was barely audible. He reached the intersection between the galley and the women's crew quarters, pausing momentarily as he imagined Marlis curled up on her bunk, her hip forming a luscious curve under the blanket. She probably slept with that E-11 in hand, long lashes fanned against her cheeks and a slight smile on her lips. What would it be like to slip in and kiss her awake?

Uminaq. He shook his head and pivoted toward the cargo bay. That woman had gotten into his blood.

He didn't bother to brighten the bay lights. He knew every square centimeter of this ship and had boxed in the muted light before. More often than not, one of his *iluq* sensed his unrest and came to join him, lending unspoken support.

A small ring of empty containers in one corner of the bay cordoned off a section of the bay for training.

Several handholds had been secured high on the wall and ceiling for use during anti-grav training, and a weapons rack held a few knives and small hand-to-hand weapons. In the corner, a punching bag had been set up, its worn padding repaired too many times to count. He rolled his shoulders and performed a few dummy punches before slamming his bare knuckles into the thing. He'd been working for about fifteen minutes when a woman's voice jarred his focus. "Mind if I join you?"

Turning, he only barely prevented his mouth from dropping open and drooling. Marlis stood there in nothing but a tank top stretched across her breasts and a loose pair of pants that hung just below her knees. He sucked in a deep breath, telling his cock to calm down.

"Trouble sleeping?" he asked.

She rubbed her wrist. "Yeah, I miss Twerp."

"Sorry Tovik's taking so long. I'll get it back for you first thing in the morning."

"Thank you. She's a pain in the ass, but you kind of get accustomed to her reporting to you all the time."

He watched her fingers encircle her slender wrist. "She?"

Marlis smiled wryly. "I know Syndicorp says computer programs don't have rights, but AIs *are* sentient, and Twerp's been my most steady friend."

There it was again; that loyalty he admired. He nodded in understanding.

She moved to the weapons rack and pulled out one of the knives, testing the blunted edge with a thumb. "You guys have a PT routine on the ship?"

"Not formally."

She tossed him the knife and picked up a second one. "How about you show me what you got?"

He grinned, widening his stance. Every cell in his body yearned to fill with power, to really show what his ionic strength could do. He tamped the urge down. Not only would he harm himself, using his abilities against a human would be unfair during training. "Think you can take me?"

She raised a brow, then spun the knife expertly between her fingers before solidifying her grip. "What do we count for points? Back on the carrier, we had electric vests that registered strikes during training."

"You're not wearing a vest." He couldn't help glancing at her chest.

She pushed her shoulders back, and by the look in her eye, he was certain she knew exactly what effect that had on him. "So, what do you suggest?"

"Practice disarming. First one to drop the weapon scrubs the galley tomorrow."

"I have a better idea." She twirled the knife. "If I win, you let me call my sister."

Between the glinting blade and the twinkle in her eyes, he was mesmerized enough to agree to almost anything. Almost. "I told you we need to wait until the captain returns."

"It doesn't have to be a two-way conversation. She has a new position and is likely to be busy, anyway. I only need to leave a message that I'm safe. I'll tell her I have an exciting new job with a cargo ship and she'll just figure I forgot to mention details."

He sighed. That was reasonable. "So, if you win, you get to call your sister. What if I win?"

She pursed her pink lips seductively and shrugged, making her breasts jiggle. "What do you want?"

He narrowed his eyes, a fire burning in his belly. He liked how direct she was about her goals; to get this job, to call her sister... to have him. *Ellam Cua*, he was staring at his perfect mate, and by the way she met his gaze, he was sure she wanted him, too. The urge to ping her again surged in his chest, but he tamped it down, growling, "Mek wouldn't approve of what I want."

"I know we're not compatible… yet. But it could be fun finding out how compatible we *might* be."

His cock surged against his fly. He made a slightly strangled sound in his throat, but he was somewhat aware of nodding like an idiot.

With a naughty grin, she lunged at him.

He regained his senses with barely enough time to twist out of the way, swinging around to spank her ass with the flat of his blade. His swipe only caught air. Facing her again, he grinned. "Feisty little *tunrak!*"

She laughed and thrust out her chin, eyes sparking. "Yes, I am."

He feinted a grab for her knife. She ducked and swept out a leg, trying to take him down. He seized her ankle, but she managed to twist free, facing him once more. They dodged and lunged for another few minutes, working up a sweat. He had to admit, she was good. She'd give anyone in Galactic Ops a run for their money.

Crouching, he coiled himself and launched forward, thinking brute force might tackle her. She brought up a knee, making contact squarely against his jaw. He saw stars, but didn't slow, carrying her to the decking.

They hit the floor hard, but she rolled out of his grasp, regaining her feet almost immediately.

"*Assirpaa!*" He gripped his knife and leaped upright to face her once again. "You must really want to call your sister."

"I do." The playfulness in her expression hardened. She lowered her guard as if about to say more.

Before she could speak, he lunged.

She must've been bluffing, because she leaped at the same moment, rolling herself across his back and locking onto his weapon hand. Hammering her knee against his arm, she tried to dislodge his knife. His hand went numb as his elbow bent the wrong way. The woman was strong and knew just where to apply pressure. But he was stronger. Flexing his biceps, he wrenched free. Before she could dodge away, he clamped both arms around her. He yanked her backward against his chest, keeping the blade of his knife pointing outward.

She elbowed him in the ribs, forcing him to exhale with a grunt. He was going to have bruises tomorrow, but he held tight. Keeping one arm locked around her waist, he used his other hand to pull her knife arm toward him. If he'd been using his powers, he'd've sent a little jolt into her arm to make her release the weapon. As it was, he had to rely on his fingers applying pressure against her tendon.

She was breathing hard, writhing against his grip, and the thin film of sweat on her skin smelled deliciously of fresh linen and musk. He breathed deeply, mesmerized by the slope of creamy skin exposed by the neck of her tank top. The way her soft hair tangled against his beard. She arched her back, panting as she attempted to wrestle free.

Her ass wiggling against him drew a different reaction than the urge to fight, however. Every flex of her muscles forced him to steady her tighter against him and made his cock grow harder. She arched again, rolling her hips downward in a way that had nothing to do with escape.

She wasn't fighting fair.

Anaq. If she was going to fight dirty, so was he. Lowering his mouth, he ran his tongue along the shell of her ear and pressed a possessive, wide-mouthed kiss against her throat, tasting the soft salty tang of her skin. She gasped and shuddered, her rolling hips freezing in place. "That's cheating!"

He wrapped his other arm around her hips, grinding his hard-on against her ass. "Is it?"

She struggled against his hold, and the scent of her arousal reached him, drowning him in pheromones and heat. Instinct rose inside him, the need to open his senses and verify she was a viable mate. Instead, he flicked his tongue against her ear once more and spread his palm flat over her ribcage, just below the weight of a breast.

"We're supposed to disarm each other," she panted. She arched her back again, centering the crack of her ass over his erection. "That's our deal."

"So, disarm me." He pressed the rounded knob of his knife's hilt into the juncture between her thighs.

She gasped and bucked, releasing a shaky breath that nearly had him undone.

Anaq. Mek was going to murder him. But Marlis was the sexiest woman this side of the galaxy, and every atom of his being urged him to make her his any way he could.

"Do you always fight this dirty?" Her voice was a husky whisper.

In answer, he flexed his hips, pressing his cock against her while sliding the smooth hilt in and out between her legs, massaging her clit through the fabric there.

She shuddered and clamped her thighs over the knob. "I'll take that as a yes."

With her free hand, she reached behind her, flattening her palm against the side of his buttock and urging him closer. Then she began a sinuous, rolling motion, pressing and releasing, pressing and releasing. He wasn't sure if she was doing it to feel his erection on her backside or to rub the knife hilt over her clit. Either reason was enough to drive him insane. Her musk filled his senses again, and he groaned.

Sliding the hand on her ribcage upward, he cupped her breast, finding the nipple hard through the material of her tank top. He rolled the bud between forefinger and thumb until it drew to exquisite tightness. She let her head loll back against his collarbone, exposing her throat, and he used his teeth to pull the strap of her tank top off her shoulder, rubbing his beard along the exposed skin.

She turned her face toward him over her shoulder, lips slightly parted, tawny eyes hooded. An invitation. He captured her lips. The need to feel her, to caress her, to taste every inch of her overwhelmed him. Flinging aside his knife, he drove his fingertips between her thighs to cup the damp heat pooling there. *Assirpaa!* How long since he'd touched a woman? And Marlis wasn't just any woman; she was perfect in every way.

In a sudden twist, she spun to face him, their lips still locked, her tongue flicking against his teeth. His blood turned to magma, his very essence on fire with need. His secondary heart slammed out a frantic counterpart to his main heart's beat. *Claim her. Claim her. Claim her.*

Resisting his ionic instinct, he focused on her needs, gripping her ass with both hands. Her body was a play of contrasts, muscles beneath soft feminine curves, strength underlying an utter submission to his ravaging tongue. He plunged into her mouth, tasting her again and again, clenching her against his chest as he devoured her.

Her fingers slid up the bare skin of his back, leaving a wake of tingling heat behind. *Ellam Cua,* he wanted her laid out naked before him. He wanted to taste every inch of her body. Leave no spot unmarked by his touch.

Sudden light filled the cargo bay, and a feminine voice echoed from the catwalk. "—perhaps we could investigate improving the torque modulator on the—"

"Noatak!" Tovik's voice drowned out the rest of the sentence. "You and Mek told me to cool it, now you're down here alone with her! That's not fair!"

Noatak released his hold on Marlis and she slipped away, a sly grin on her face. She brandished her knife toward the one he'd thrown to the deck. "I think I won our bet."

He couldn't help the smile curling his lips. "Feisty little *tunrak*."

Chapter Nine

Marlis tried to act cool, but her legs were still wobbly from the intensity of Noatak's kiss. She'd intended to enjoy a little banter, perhaps some suggestive touching, but in no way had she expected him to take the lead as he did. She was usually the driving force in a relationship, and she felt off-balance, not to mention ready to strip naked and let Noatak have his way with her—nanites or no nanites.

She lifted her gaze from Noatak's broad, naked chest to the catwalk. Tovik was probably in shock after seeing what they'd been doing. She cleared her throat. "Hey, Tovik."

Tovik's eyes were filled with a disappointment that reminded her of an abandoned puppy. He raised his hand, the wristband with her AI dangling from his fingertips. "I checked out your AI. She's clean." Shooting Noatak a disgusted look, he jumped to the lower deck next to them and handed Marlis the band. "There you go, Twerp, back where you belong."

Twerp replied, "Thank you, Tovik."

"You're welcome." Tovik shifted his attention from the band to Marlis. "I disabled her wireless sensor. You no longer have spatial data or a locator, but the ship's small, so Twerp thinks you should be okay."

"I provided Tovik all my assistance parameters," Twerp said.

Marlis swallowed. That meant he knew everything that was wrong with her. It had been bound to come to light, anyway. "That's fine, Twerp."

Tovik's mouth quirked into an indulgent half-smile. "Twerp, if you can talk Marlis into giving you a visual sensor, let me know. I have some ideas."

Marlis strapped her AI onto her wrist and smiled at the young man. "It's bad enough she butts in on everything I say. I don't need her looking over my shoulder, too."

Noatak chuckled, turning away to retrieve the knife he'd tossed to the deck.

Tovik tilted his head. "She's sentient, you know. Think how much happier she'd be if she could see."

Twerp chimed, "Thank you, Tovik. I am sentient. However, all Syndicorp sanctioned AIs are required to include programming protocols to restrict autonomy. This is to prevent an AI from intentionally harming a human being. I have long contemplated the idea of free will—"

"Enough, Twerp." Marlis said, shaking her wrist. "You and Tovik can discuss philosophy later."

Noatak held out a hand for her knife and she handed it over, heat flooding her again as she recalled the hilt of his weapon between her thighs. He returned both weapons to the rack. "You ready to send a message to your sister?"

"Thanks for taking care of Twerp, Tovik." With a parting smile, she followed Noatak up the steps and down the hall. They reached the small ship's cockpit-sized bridge. Hard to believe this closet was the command center. Noatak gestured toward the chair on the right and lowered his massive frame into the seat on the opposite side, his head nearly brushing the ceiling. A vast view screen on the wall made it feel like she was standing outside in space.

Tapping the console, Noatak pulled up the comm system. "This is the only place on the ship with access to external communications. After you've recorded your message, I'll need to strip the identification coding and we can send it."

She smiled, grateful to be able to tell her sister she was safe and had a job, and looked straight into the screen. "Hey, Attie! Good news. I got a position on a small cargo ship. We're still near the station, waiting to rendezvous with another ship, and then we're off. Things are going well so far..." She flicked a glance at Noatak, heat creeping up her face. His expression was unreadable, and she wondered what he was thinking. *Stay focused on Attie.*

Leaning closer to the screen, she said, "I can't wait to tell you all about it. Oh, and just so you know, Dad tried to sabotage me, so I'm not speaking to him at the moment. If you talk to him, tell him he's an asshole."

She cut the recording and looked at Noatak. He took over the comm, fingers flying over the control panel as he encoded the message and sent it.

"Thank you," Marlis said.

He nodded, seemingly unable to meet her gaze. "You should get some rest. It's been a long day."

"For both of us." Had she said or done something to upset him? All she remembered was the feel of his hands on her body. But she'd done things to offend people before without realizing it. She twisted her wristband. Now that she had Twerp back to help her understand things, it was time to talk to the doctor about the nanites fixing her memory. "You think Mek's awake yet?"

He watched her hands, then lifted his gaze to hers. "You want to talk about the nanites?"

A twinge of heat ran through her core. Although her primary goal for the nanites was to heal her brain, the things were related to mating in Noatak's mind. And if the cargo bay had been any indication, he was primed and ready to help her wrap things up in that department. "Do you think I should take them?"

His face twitched, and he worked his jaw as if fighting back what he really wanted to say. "What I think is irrelevant."

"But I respect your opinion." She tilted her head, wondering why he was being so evasive.

He stroked his beard and sighed. "One thing Mek never mentioned is that humans and denaidans who mate appear to forge a permanent bond. You will likely be unable to pair with anyone else ever again."

She laughed. "As in soul mates? That's not a real thing."

He continued to look into her eyes somberly, as if daring her to doubt him again.

She quieted. "Wait, you're serious?"

"Completely. You can talk to Joy or Lisa about it if you want to know what it's like for a human."

"Popular science asserts the occurrence of 'true mates' is merely a psychological affinity," Twerp added. "However, several studies seem to indicate some species are capable of developing a symbiosis which ties their life forces together. While scientific theory has not yet been able to empirically measure—"

"Okay, Twerp," Marlis said, her brain already overflowing. "Thank you."

Noatak rose from the chair and ducked into the hallway. "If you want to come with me, I can get Mek's data for you."

"Thank you," Twerp said. "I appreciate all forms of information, particularly when it may be of assistance to Marlis."

"He was talking to me, Twerp." Marlis pushed out of the chair and trailed after Noatak to the med bay. Why did he seem so sad? She'd think he'd be excited she might accept the nanites.

He stepped inside and retrieved a polycom. "This has all his files on the nanites." Handing it over, he moved to the door before adding, "You'll get to meet the rest of the crew soon. Please think carefully before you say yes. Once you're inoculated, there's only one way to clear your system."

Without a backward glance at her, he disappeared around the corner.

Was he saying he wasn't interested? They'd just gotten hot and heavy in the cargo bay, and there'd been no denying the erection she'd felt through his clothes. Maybe he wasn't interested in forming a commitment. Not that she'd be looking, either, if this nanite thing hadn't come up. But if she was going to have to choose someone to bond with, Noatak would be a good option. Not just good, amazing. He liked guns as much as she did and had been so understanding with her when she'd been forced to recall Pulati. She was also pretty sure he could take her in a hand-to-hand match if they actually followed the rules. *Be logical, Marlis.* What did he get out of a union except a ball-and-chain?

It only took her one wrong turn to find her way back to her bunk. Luckily, without ending up in Tovik's bedroom or something. Trying not to wake Emmy, she plugged Twerp into the polycom before falling into a restless sleep. What felt like moments later, Emmy's alarm brought her wide awake.

Rolling toward the edge of the bed, Marlis watched Emmy rise and stretch. Emmy noticed she was awake. "Where'd you go last night?"

Marlis flushed with heat. She slid from the bunk to the floor, shivering as the cold deck contacted her bare feet. "Uh, sparring with Noatak."

All traces of sleep left Emmy's face. "Sparring, huh?" She winked. "That why you're blushing?"

Something close to a giggle rose in Marlis's throat. *A giggle?* She didn't giggle. Not even with Attie. Maybe Twerp was right. She could use a human friend. With a small shrug, she said, "Things did get a little… personal."

"Did you kiss him?" Emmy grabbed her hand and pulled her onto the bottom bunk, crossing her legs to face her. "Was it amazing? Who could've imagined aliens could be so hot?"

This time, Marlis did laugh. She pulled her legs in, mimicking Emmy's cross-legged posture, so they sat knee-to-knee. "They're certainly not tentacle-faced posungi."

Emmy cocked her head, face alight. "So... are all his parts in the right places? How far'd you get?"

"Not that far." Heat was pooling low in her abdomen as she remembered just how well he'd lined up to her ass. "Humans and denaidans can't have sex."

Disappointment creased Emmy's face. "Really? I thought Joy was married to one of the captains."

Marlis shook her head, trying to put the pieces she remembered into sentences. Slowly, she explained about the nanites and how they were going to fix her. "But that's not what they were meant to do. They actually have something to do with denaidan mating, which can be deadly to humans without the nanites."

"So your AI was right? This is a sex thing, and they brought us on board to create mates?" Emmy shrank back, her eyes wide.

"No, I don't think Mek would've even told me about the nanites except for my brain damage. I think he just keeps them on hand in case people want to... you know, get together. I mean, it would be bad to not have something available, wouldn't it?"

Emmy seemed to relax and nodded thoughtfully. "Good point."

Twerp chimed from the top bunk. "I have completed my analysis, Marlis. Would you like me to explain?"

"That would be great, Twerp." She rose and retrieved the wristband, strapping it back in place before settling down.

While Twerp went over the information Mek had provided earlier and Emmy asked questions, Marlis's mind wandered back to the cargo bay. Why wouldn't Noatak want to bond with her? They both liked guns. He seemed to want to protect people as much as she did. And they were in this resistance together, which from the sound of it was just beginning. Assuming Syndicorp didn't discover them and shut everything down before it even had a chance to begin, they were looking at years of working together. Maybe she needed to prove herself to him first. But Mek had said time was of the essence here…

"Are you going to?" Emmy's voice yanked her out of her thoughts.

"Going to? Oh." She cleared her throat, realizing she hadn't heard a word Twerp'd said. "Twerp, are they safe?"

"Nanites are not an approved medical treatment for your type of brain injury, Marlis. The procedure is purely experimental."

"I know it's experimental, but if there's a chance of fixing me, I should take it."

"It is theoretically possible for nano technology to repair damage to your central nervous system. However, previous test subjects had to be closely monitored to prevent adverse side effects. My primary function is to support your wellness. In the event you choose to accept the nanites, I will need Tovik's assistance recalibrating my biometric sensors to continue monitoring you."

"So you're saying go ahead?"

"If that is your decision, I will assist in any way I can."

Emmy gaped at her. "You're okay with... with the end part?"

Marlis shrugged, her face heating. "If it's anything like last night with Noatak, then hell yes."

Twerp spoke up. "Humans are notoriously promiscuous, therefore I would not theorize that every pairing would result in a symbiotic bond. I have been comparing the data Mek provided alongside other scientific studies about symbiotic life-bonds in various species. The data on human-denaidan pairings reflects an insignificant amount of information to arrive at a statistical conclusion."

Emmy laughed. "Okay, then."

"Will you go with me to see Mek?" Although Marlis was used to going to appointments alone, this nanite thing was unfamiliar territory. It'd be good to have someone besides Twerp to provide input. "He said there may be side effects and stuff. It'd be nice to have you there."

"Of course!" Emmy beamed at her. "Who knows? Maybe someday I'll ask the same thing of you. These denaidans are pretty tempting. Even Tovik's kinda cute."

A knock at the door halted the conversation as Tovik's voice came from outside. "I made you both breakfast!"

"Be right there!" Emmy called quickly, her face turning pink.

"Okay, Emmy!" Tovik's muffled voice answered.

Pointing toward the door, Emmy silently mouthed, "Think he heard me?"

Repressing her laughter, Marlis slid out of the bunk and grabbed her pants. "I suppose breakfast would be a good idea before I talk to Mek."

Emmy joined her, pulling off her pajama top. Once they were dressed, they headed to the galley where Tovik had attempted to make pancakes. "Lisa says these are human comfort food," he said as he placed plates on the table. The little disks were stiff, misshapen, and required some chewing, but Marlis gulped down a bite while he hovered. "Do you like them?"

"Mmm," Marlis replied, taking a large swig of coffee to wash it down. At least the coffee was hot and not too weak.

"You did a fine job for your first time," Emmy said, pouring more syrup onto her plate.

"I'd be happy to make them for you again." He sat down to his own plate and cut into one. His grin faded. "These are nothing like Lisa's."

"Pancakes take practice," Emmy said.

He sighed and reached for the butter. "You're too nice."

After they helped clean up, Marlis led Emmy to the med bay. Mek was inside rearranging items in a cupboard. He turned and smiled, his gaze cautious. "Good morning, ladies. Everything all right?"

"I've decided to take the nanites." Marlis moved into the bay. "Emmy's here as moral support."

"You told her?" Mek's hands froze around the tube he was coiling.

Emmy took a spot on the opposite side of the table. "Actually, Twerp told me."

Marlis held up her wrist. "Noatak gave me the data last night, and I fed the files to Twerp. She says I should go ahead."

"I believe my actual response was that I will support your decision but will need to be recalibrated if I am to assist with your treatment," Twerp said. "It is a pleasure to make your acquaintance, doctor."

"Likewise." Mek raised his eyebrows. "I'm sure Tovik would be happy to help modify your programming. Having an AI monitor biometrics will be quite valuable. You understand the side effects and requirements?"

"Yes," both Twerp and Marlis responded at once. Twerp

vibrated gently against Marlis's wrist, which Marlis always took as a form of laughter in instances like this.

Mek opened a cabinet and pulled out a vial. "You're quite sure about this?"

Marlis nodded, her heartbeat quickening. "If there's a chance to fix my brain, I'm all in."

"All right," Mek gestured to the exam table. "Lie back and I'll begin the injection."

Closing her eyes, Marlis waited for the magic to begin.

CHAPTER TEN

After his interlude with Marlis, Noatak spent a long, sleepless night thinking. He was relieved she hadn't accepted the nanites off the cuff. He wasn't usually the kind of guy to get his hopes up, but Marlis was one hell of a woman, and one he'd consider worth hoping for. Perhaps Mek could find a cure for his ionic heart while she considered. He'd finally fallen into a fitful sleep when the comm woke him with news the *Kinship* had returned.

Jaw cracking around an enormous yawn, he rose and scrubbed his face with hot water before dressing and heading to the cargo bay to meet the crew. He'd barely made it to the bottom of the cargo bay stairs when Kashatok was in his face. "You left her!"

Bowing his head, Noatak crossed his arms. He deserved this, but that didn't mean he had to like it. "The place was getting under my skin. I needed air."

"You guaranteed her safety!" Kashatok shoved him.

Noatak braced himself and prepared for more blows. If someone'd let his mate get hurt, he'd be pissed, too.

Joy moved in behind Kashatok, laying a hand on his shoulder. "Calm down. I told you I'm fine."

Kashatok glowered at Noatak another moment, ionic power rolling off him in waves, then spun and stalked to a cluster of men who were helping offload supplies. Chignik, the *Kinship's* main gunner, glanced toward the catwalk above Noatak's head. "There they are!"

Taking two steps, he leaped to the catwalk, Ekwok mere seconds behind him. Noatak spun to look overhead, spotting several sets of feet on the grating.

"Hey!" Tovik's voice echoed loud through the bay as he launched himself after them.

Then Marlis's voice joined the mix, "Back off, assholes!"

Without using his ionic powers, Noatak raced up the stairs three at a time. "Get your asses back down to the deck before you clumsy *terpaks* knock our new crew members off the catwalk."

"I just wanted to say hi," Chignik complained, swinging an elbow at Tovik in a less-than-friendly manner. "You guys got a head start."

Tovik put his hands on his hips. "I've hardly got to talk to them at all yet."

Ekwok sighed and trudged to the stairs, turning to look longingly over his shoulder. "Which one's coming to our ship?"

Noatak's chest ached at the possibility Marlis might join the other crew. Stepping aside to allow Ekwok to pass, Noatak said, "None of them if you two keep acting like idiots."

A sharp whistle from below was followed by Captain Kashatok's voice. "Everyone on deck for a debrief."

Chignik grumbled as he moved to the stairs. Tovik grinned triumphantly until Noatak raised his eyebrows. "That means you, too, Tovik."

"I know," the kid said, beckoning the women with one hand. "I'm just showing our new crew members the way."

"You think they're going to get lost?"

"I'm being a gentleman," Tovik said as he passed. Next time Noatak had the kid alone, he was going to have to discuss the difference between chivalry and chauvinism.

Marlis brushed her fingertips along the top of Noatak's hand as she passed, whether or not intentionally, he wasn't sure, but his ionic senses flared to life before he could seal off the reaction. He took a deep breath and clamped down on his control. He should step out of the running. Tell her he wasn't interested. Even Tovik was a better bet than he was. Yet his chest ached with desire at every twitch of her hips as she moved toward the group of waiting men.

Qaiyaan waited at the bottom of the stairs and clapped a hand to his shoulder. "These the only two?"

"Aye, Captain." Noatak nodded and cut a glance toward Joy. Thank *Ellam Cua* she was upright and functional. "Whylon Station didn't go as well as planned."

"I heard." Qaiyaan sighed. "Kashatok aborted our reconnaissance as soon as he found out."

"How'd he find out?"

"The kid." Qaiyaan tilted his head toward Tovik, who

was watching Chignik and Ekwok jostle for the spot next to Emmy. "Couldn't you rein him in?"

Of course it was the kid. They'd all sworn to protect Joy, but Tovik thought that meant informing her mate of anything that went awry, regardless of the consequences to the larger mission. "I'll have a talk with him."

Qaiyaan nodded and moved to the circle of cargo containers they'd pulled over as seats for the meeting. At least no one appeared to be bothering Marlis, possibly because of the pistol at her hip. He had no doubt she'd use it if anyone got too bold.

As if sensing his scrutiny, she turned her head to look over her shoulder at him and their gazes connected like lightning. A slight twitch of her head was all the invitation he needed to stride forward. But a bob of her head indicated he should take a seat on Emmy's other side.

Uminaq. He wanted to sit next to Marlis, find excuses to brush his shoulder against hers or touch her knee. But he also understood her need to protect her friend from these over-eager louts. *Ellam Cua.* She had him wrapped around her finger and didn't even know it. With one arm, he shoved both men aside and sat next to Emmy.

Chignik and Ekwok ceased arguing and gaped at him.

"What the hell, *iluq?*" Chignik asked.

Qaiyaan cut short any argument. "Just take a damned seat. Now's not the time for fraternizing."

Tovik crossed his arms and glared at Noatak. "Exactly when is a good time, then?"

Noatak glared back.

Chignik took a spot on Marlis's other side. Jealousy flared inside Noatak's gut and he narrowed his eyes at the big gunner. Shooting Noatak a grin as wide as a rakwiji bounty hunter's, Chignik turned his attention toward Marlis. "Hey."

Marlis barely glanced at him, her focus on Qaiyaan in the center of the ring of containers. "Hey."

Noatak smirked and turned toward the captain as well.

Emmy leaned close to him. "Are all denaidan men this... big?"

Glancing down at her, he realized her petite frame was barely half the size of the nearby men. Maybe he should make size a consideration during the next round of interviews. "Yes," he answered.

Qaiyaan nodded toward Marlis and Emmy. "We're happy to have you on board. My name's Qaiyaan. I'm captain of the *Hardship*. Everyone, take a quick moment to introduce yourself."

As everyone spoke, Noatak could tell by Marlis's face she was panicking. He pulled out his polycom. "There'll be information about the mission. I need to take notes."

Marlis cast him a grateful glance and pulled out her polycom.

Chignik leaned closer to her. "Chignik, with a C. In case you wondered."

She shook her head and edged away to enter something into her polycom. Noatak hoped it said 'asshole'.

Once the introductions were concluded, Qaiyaan asked, "Do I need to catch our newcomers up about the nanites, or are they already informed?"

Noatak's stomach roiled. Once the men knew Marlis was first in line to take the nanites, they'd be all over her. He opened his mouth to speak, but Mek beat him to it. "They do. I inoculated Marlis a few hours ago."

Every denaidan crew member in the bay focused on Marlis. Noatak sucked in a breath. When had she taken them? And why hadn't Mek informed him? *Because you're not in the running, terpak.*

Ekwok pointed toward Mek while looking at Kashatok. "I told you their crew would take unfair advantage!"

Chignik jumped to his feet, menace rolling off him in waves. "You should've waited until we returned."

Tovik gaped, rising and glaring at Noatak. "How long has she had them?"

Noatak forced himself to remain sitting, although every cell in his body wanted to get up and stake his claim—now. A claim he could never make. His attraction to Marlis was making him want to act like a beast in rut.

"Get your men under control, captain," Qaiyaan growled at Kashatok.

Kashatok thrust a finger toward Tovik. "Soon as you get control of yours."

From the corner of his eye, Noatak saw Marlis's hand slide toward her holster.

Mek had moved into the circle. "Calm down. The nanites were only administered a few hours ago. I didn't know how soon the Kinship would return, and the sample was deteriorating rapidly. I had to act."

"Why? So you could have her all to yourself?" Chignik stepped within swinging distance of the doctor.

"I'm her doctor." Mek seemed to swell. "I have no intentions toward Marlis."

"Put her on our ship, then," Chignik said. The room churned with testosterone and raw power.

Marlis's palm brushed her weapon. The women were safe, but she wouldn't understand that; the rest of the crew might go back to their bunks with bruises, but the women would never be harmed.

Leaning across Emmy's lap, Noatak put a hand on Marlis's knee, surprised by the tiny shock that raced up his arm. Once more, his ionic senses flared without his volition. Now that he knew she had the nanites, he could detect the subtle change within her, like the scent of freshly fallen rain. *Down, boy.* His powers were no longer only dangerous to himself; a ping could cause the nanites to react badly. Both Lisa and Joy had experienced blackouts when they'd had them.

"It's okay," he said. "Mek's got this."

After a moment, she nodded and moved her hand back to her lap, fingers curling and uncurling as if fighting a leash.

A sharp whistle brought everyone to silence. Qaiyaan stood on top of one container, his hands on his hips.

"I'm about to throw you three in the brig." Tovik opened his mouth to argue, but Qaiyaan silenced him with a look. "Yes, you too. Now, let the doctor finish his report."

It took every ounce of Noatak's will to turn his attention back to Mek.

The doctor put his hands on his hips. "I'll be monitoring Marlis closely with the aid of her AI, Twerp." He turned to Marlis. "Twerp, please say hello."

"G-greetings." The chirpy voice on Marlis's wrist spoke a strange hiccup. "I'm pleased to make your acquaintance." Marlis had said the thing was sentient, but it was funny to think the AI might be nervous.

Mek continued, "The nanites will be performing some ancillary tasks while replicating. It's too early to tell how quickly we might be able to collect a new supply."

Qaiyaan moved to the center of the circle. "Hopefully soon. Marlis may be our only source of nanites for a good long while."

Tovik groaned. "The lab wasn't under the mine on Zyrinic Eight?"

"It was until they moved it," Kashatok said. "The corp

installed a huge Faraday cage on one of their flagships and appears to be operating from there."

Lisa added, "They've probably moved out of stage two testing. The corp always planned to use cyber-sensitive technology in their espionage activities, and a mobile lab opens up territory."

"We're better at boarding ships than ground assaults." Tovik said, glancing at the assembled men. "Shouldn't this be good news?"

"Only if we can find the ship," Qaiyaan answered. "The *Icarus* is equipped with the very latest cloaking technology. The running joke is that not even the corp knows where it's at."

"I'm working on the intel, but it's going to take some time," Kashatok said. "And it isn't cheap. We're going to need to take on some jobs in the meantime. I have a lead on a payload of corp computer hardware moving to one of the new manufacturing colonies. The ship'll be ripe for the picking if we can get our asses in gear in time to intercept."

Tovik let out a whoop. "New hardware!"

"To sell, Tovik. We've got to pay for intel, remember?" Noatak reminded him. The kid was always disassembling perfectly good equipment to fashion what he called "prototype" technology. Most of it never worked the way he expected.

"We can keep a few things, though, right?" Tovik looked hopefully toward Qaiyaan.

Qaiyaan sighed. "We'll see." He panned his gaze over the assembled crew. "Now that we're bringing on new crew members, I expect all of you to be on your best behavior. This isn't some gladiator ring where the winner gets the girl. Understood?"

The men mumbled, and Chignik looked at Qaiyaan from beneath his brows. "It's not fair to our crew if the girls are both over here. Since Mek needs to keep an eye on the nanites, at least send the other girl to the *Kinship*."

"Her name's Emmy." Marlis rose, her hand once more on the butt of her pistol. This time, Noatak didn't stop her. She'd need to prove herself to these men eventually. Might as well start now.

She shoved a finger in Chignik's face. "And if all you're looking for is mates, I suggest you take out an ad with one of the dating agencies. Both Emmy and I are here to join the revolution, not be passed around like blow-up dolls."

Chignik had the courtesy to flush and lowered his gaze. "I meant no disrespect."

The rest of the crew laughed at his discomfort, and Qaiyaan nodded, his gaze sliding to Noatak with unspoken approval in his eyes. Ekwok slapped Chignik on the shoulder. "Don't be an *ucuk*."

Marlis went back to her seat, and Qaiyaan spoke once more. "New crew members need to remain here until Mek clears them. Once the *Kinship* has its own doctor, that might change. For now, Kashatok's crew is welcome to serve rotations over here so everyone can get to know each other. Noatak will set up a work schedule for shift rotation."

Much as Noatak wanted to refuse the task, he nodded. A rotation was only fair, and he couldn't have Marlis, anyway. Perhaps the sooner she moved her attention to another male, the better.

Chapter Eleven

Sitting in the confines of the laser turret, Marlis went over the targeting layout for what felt like the hundredth time. Part of her was concerned about stealing a ship full of computer parts, but she kept reminding herself it was a Syndicorp ship, and Syndicorp was the bad guy. At least her memory was clear about that. Acknowledging the truth had rocked her to the core at first, but with her suspicions confirmed, every jumbled memory had clicked into place—if only her short-term memories had followed. But the nanites were going to fix that.

She zeroed in on a cargo container Noatak'd ejected for her to use as target practice and fired. The shot barely nicked the corner, setting the box spinning. Dammit, she was better than this. She'd studied ship-mounted weapons on Syndicorp carriers, freighters, and even practiced for a gunner seat on a small fighter ship. But the *Hardship's* systems were antiquated and less automated than she was used to. She couldn't seem to hold the range ignition order in her head.

"I thought these nanites were supposed to be improving my memory," she grumbled to herself. For three days they'd been waiting for signs the nanites had become active. She'd hoped to have at least a little memory improvement by now.

Twerp buzzed soothingly against her wrist. "The doctor said the process could take some time, Marlis. I am not yet d-detecting significant neural changes in your biometric data."

Twerp had developed a strange hiccup since Tovik had recalibrated her. Marlis paused her task and tapped the AI. "Twerp, put a reminder on my calendar to take you back to Tovik for a check."

"Of course."

A set of broad shoulders pushed up through the hatch, topped by a head of braided hair. For some reason, she kept wanting to call this guy Jake-with-a-J, but knew that wasn't right. He grinned at her. "Need any help in here?"

Shaking her head, she said, "I got this, thanks."

"You might appreciate a hand from an expert." He winked and pulled himself higher into the small turret.

She'd met his kind before, men who thought women couldn't possibly handle the big guns. Before he could step off the ladder, she swiveled the chair, her knees forcing him to lean backward against the starboard view screen. He laid his hands on her thighs, ostensibly to steady himself, but she didn't like the way his fingers squeezed, as if he was just itching to cop a feel. Keeping her legs closed so there'd be no mistake, Marlis rammed her knees hard into his abdomen. "I don't need you in here man-splaining. When I need a hand, I'll ask, okay?"

"Okay, okay, I get it." He raised his hands in surrender. She eased up the pressure and his grin returned. "But you need anything, I'm here for you. I like a woman who knows her way around a turret."

Turning back to the controls, she let out a short breath, keeping a tight hold on her anger as he retreated. Fuck, these guys were hard up. If it wasn't Tovik, it was this guy, or the other dude with sandy hair. Even the old-timer in the other ship's engineering bay had winked at her. She was growing tired of always needing to fend someone off. *Everyone but Noatak.*

The First Mate seemed to be the one man keeping his distance. It was as if he wanted to give the other men room to move in, which baffled her, especially since she kept catching his eyes on her. Thinking about him now ignited heat low in her pelvis as if his touch there had started a fire that refused to go out. She didn't even want to think about anyone else's hands on her.

Twerp let out a long buzz. "You have an appointment with the doctor in half an hour, Marlis."

Sighing, she shut down the targeting system and climbed out of the turret. Hopefully, today there was good news. On the way to find the doc, she spotted Noatak ducking into the weapons locker. She paused and poked her head inside. "Can I talk to you a minute?"

He turned stiffly away from the weapons bench. "What is it?"

She glanced over her shoulder toward the cargo bay where Tovik and the guy from the turret were working on something. Although they weren't outright looking at her, she could feel their attention, nonetheless. Perhaps it was the nanites. She didn't care. All she wanted was to clear the air with Noatak, and this was the closest to alone she'd been with him in three days.

She stepped inside the narrow cage and shut the door, knowing it wouldn't give her any real privacy, but needing to at least pretend they weren't being watched. "Are you avoiding me?"

He stared at her for several heartbeats before answering. "I'm giving you space."

"I don't remember asking for space. At least not from you."

His posture shifted a fraction. "Is someone treating you badly?"

"Not exactly." She shrugged. "But the men are driving me crazy, trying to get my attention. I know you guys are looking for mates, but I'm not interested. At least…" she licked her lips, suddenly nervous, "not in them. Can you just claim me or something and make them leave me alone?"

He rubbed the back of his neck, eyes filled with what she could only interpret as pain. "I can't."

Her breath caught. She hadn't expected him to say no. "I don't understand. The other night in the practice ring—"

"That was a mistake. I shouldn't have taken things that far." Shoulders stiff, he took one step sideways as if to move around her toward the door. "Give these other men a chance."

"A mistake?" She intercepted him, one hand against his chest. "Hell, no. I don't know what's going on with this 'fairness' bullshit, but I'm interested in you. Only you. What do I have to do to make you want me?"

She was close enough to feel the warmth coming off of his body. He let out a shaky breath. *"Ellam Cua,* Marlis. It's not that I don't want you."

Lifting up on her toes, she brought her face closer to his and looked determinedly into his eyes. "So, what's the problem?"

His breath fanned her cheek, and she could see desire in his gunmetal blue gaze. "If we bond, I'll most likely leave you a widow."

She scowled. "You think I'm just going to sit around and let you do all the fighting on your own? Who's to say I wouldn't take a bullet first?"

A smirk lifted one side of his mouth. "Feisty little *tunrak.*" He reached up to brush a strand of loose hair from her cheek, sending sparks of heat straight through her middle. The moment ended too soon as he dropped his hand and cleared his throat. "But I'm not talking about a gunfight. My ionic heart is on the edge of failure. It's only a matter of time before it gives out completely. Mating would probably kill me." His voice grew gravelly over the words, as if admitting the weakness had sapped him of strength. He gave her a weak, half-hearted smile. "And while dying in your arms might be a nice way to go, you deserve more."

She dropped back to her heels, pulse hammering through her ears. "But you seem perfectly healthy!" More than healthy. He exuded maleness that made her knees wobbly. Twerp had begun buzzing in response to her increased blood pressure. "There has to be a way to fix you!"

"Not that Mek's aware of." Sighing, Noatak moved backward, putting space between them. "Give the other *terpaks* a chance. They're not too bad once you get to know them."

"My memory isn't the greatest, but I'm pretty sure *terpak* means asshole." She crossed her arms. "Not a very high recommendation, if you ask me."

A half-smile lifted a corner of his mouth and he shrugged. "You're right, but I count myself among them."

The back of her eyes pricked with girly tears and she gritted her teeth to fight them back. She'd been through hell to get this job, started what could be a dangerous procedure to fix her memory, and found a guy who actually appreciated her love of guns. Just when she thought everything was looking up, it all fell apart. *Not all of it.* She was still getting her brain fixed. Noatak had simply been a cherry on top, making the whole thing complete.

"I'm not willing to give up yet." She stepped forward until her breasts nearly brushed his chest, all but pinning him against the weapons bench behind him. "My mom always said 'it ain't over until the fat lady sings', and I don't even hear music yet. The nanites haven't started replicating, which means Mek has time to find a remedy for your ionic heart."

His eyes grew dark. "You are one tenacious woman."

She lifted her chin, her mouth within an inch of his. "I know what I want."

"Irresistible," he murmured. His hands met her waist, drawing her in as he leaned down to brush his lips against hers.

Lightning coursed through her system. Noatak jolted, as if feeling it, too, and his arms engulfed her, wrapping her in his masculine scent. She relaxed her lips, allowing his tongue to explore. His thighs were like rocks against hers, and she could feel his growing arousal against her lower abdomen.

She ran one hand along his jaw, the coarse fringe of his beard tickling her fingertips while she rolled her tongue against his. He tasted like a breath of clean air after a long shuttle ride, a promise of freedom and possibility. Wrapping her other arm around his waist, she pressed her body against his, gripping the solid muscles of his lower back. Her racing heart was making it hard to breathe, but she didn't want to stop. Never, ever stop.

He threaded one large hand into the hair at the back of her scalp and tugged her head to one side, burying his face against the side of her neck. Her skin seemed to come alive under the prickle of his beard, waves of electric heat flowing down her neck and chest until her nipples burned against her bra. His teeth latched onto her earlobe, and a shiver rocked her, spasming her core as if he'd just connected to every erogenous zone in her body.

"Oh, God," she breathed, clutching the back of his neck like a lifeline. Slipping her other hand over his pants, she palmed the hard, thick roll of his erection. He was huge. Throbbing. Hot. Her pussy responded with a pulsating heat of its own, and she flexed her hips to press herself against his thigh. He groaned in her ear, trailing kisses down her throat.

They'd begun rocking against each other, an increasing storm brewing between them that could only be satiated by one thing. Her mind was fuzzy with desire, a need for him that blocked out every other concern. She fumbled for his belt, needing to touch his skin, to wrap her fingers around his shaft, circle his waist with both legs, fill herself with his heat.

Twerp buzzed hard enough to sting her skin. "Marlis, I have d-detected a sharp spike in your temperature. This may be indicative of an adverse reaction to the nanites. Please seek the doctor's attention at once."

She shook her wrist, silencing the annoyance, but Noatak pushed her away, breathing hard. "*Anaq*. Kissing can cause the nanites to react. I shouldn't have let you get this close to me."

Twerp buzzed again. "I have alerted Mek to the situation. He is expecting you."

"Dammit, Twerp." It felt like she'd been waiting months for Noatak to touch her, and now this. "I feel fine. Really."

Noatak put his hands on her shoulders and turned her toward the door. "Twerp's right." His voice was thick. "We can't take chances. I'll escort you."

Normally, she'd be angry at the insinuation she needed help, but her legs were wobbly with desire, and she wasn't about to tell him to go away. "Thank you."

Taking his hand, she led him from the weapons locker. He chuckled as he followed behind her.

"What's so funny?"

"I was supposed to escort you, not the other way around."

She didn't allow her steps to falter. "Whatever. I want to ask Mek about fixing you, anyway."

They paused outside the door to the med bay. Mek flicked a glance at their linked hands, face impassive, but his words were colder than usual. "Twerp told me you were coming. Thank you for dropping her off, Noatak. I'll take it from here."

Marlis squeezed Noatak's hand tighter. "I want him to stay. I have some questions about his ionic heart condition."

Mek's eyebrows shot up and he looked straight at Noatak. "You told her?"

Noatak nodded. "Now it's your job to convince her I'm not fixable."

"Stop saying that." She glowered at Noatak.

Twerp said, "I would be very interested in learning about d-denaidan physiology, doctor, especially since Marlis will be working among you."

"Let's deal with one thing at a time, okay? You said her immune system has engaged?" Mek pulled the large scanner over to the exam table. "Marlis, please sit."

Marlis took a seat on the table, and Noatak released her hand to give the doctor room while Twerp provided a report. "Her white blood cell count is approaching levels which may forecast a developing autoimmune cascade."

Mek adjusted the scanner over her head. "This may hurt."

He gave her that same warning every time, but she'd never felt anything more than a warming vibration, much like Twerp's reminders. She closed her eyes anyway, envisioning the nanites inside her putting the puzzle pieces of her brain back together.

After a few moments, Mek grunted, and Marlis opened her eyes to find him frowning darkly at the scanner. Her breathing sharpened. "What is it?"

"Your immune system is definitely up in arms." He shook his head. "The nanites not only aren't replicating, but their overall saturation seems to have decreased. I'm worried your immune system might destroy the nanites before they take hold."

Twerp chimed in, "Since the nanites are supposed to integrate with Marlis's system much like an organ transplant, the medically suggested course of action for humans would be to administer anti-rejection medication."

Mek rubbed his temple. "I've thought of that. But it would make her susceptible to other infections and require a period of quarantine."

"Quarantine?" Marlis sat up straighter. "You mean put me in lockdown? God, no." She'd been in solitary confinement twice back on the carrier after losing her temper during therapy sessions, trapped with nothing but her own anger and heavy medication. She never wanted to experience anything like that again.

"This is the last of our nanites." Noatak put a hand on her shoulder. "You have to protect them."

She swallowed, mollified by his touch. *Protect the nanites.* It wasn't a gunfight, but it was an important job, not only for her own sake, but for the sake of an entire species. She grimaced and stared at the bare, slate gray wall across from her. "As long as I can keep Twerp with me, fine."

"I'm not ready to take that step yet," Mek said. "The scans don't show any increase in nanite concentrations, but perhaps that's merely because they're analyzing or fixing your synaptic pathways. I want to run another round of scans before we make any decisions." He pulled the scanner close. "Lie back, please."

Marlis did as he asked, but this time kept her eyes open, watching the doctor's face as he read the screen.

Mek tapped a few keys. Moving the scanner, he tapped a few more. His face had a strangely pale sheen she hoped was just a reflection from the scanner's screen. Finally, he shut down the screen and slid the entire unit back toward the wall. "I'm not seeing any new dendrite clusters."

"What are dendrite clusters?" Marlis asked, nausea roiling below her ribs.

"The physical connections within your brain."

"So what does that mean? More waiting?"

Mek met her gaze. "I'm afraid the nanites in your system are below viable levels. They're not going to fix you."

The air felt suddenly too heavy, as if a corpse had just collapsed on top of her. She flailed one arm toward Noatak, needing someone, something to ground her. Twerp buzzed at her wrist.

"The nanites are dead." Noatak's voice was a flat monotone, so calm it was frightening. "Right?"

"Technically, machines cannot die…" Twerp began.

But Marlis could no longer hear. The nanites had died under her care. Was she somehow responsible?

Chapter Twelve

Noatak held Marlis's hand while Mek took a sample of her spinal fluid to confirm his suspicions. The nanites were dead, no more than inert microscopic bits of debris. He felt almost numb, as if the hope the nanites had provided had been a dream. Some part of him had clung to the belief there was a fix for his ionic heart and the possibility of a future. With the nanites gone, there was no hope for him, no healing for Marlis, and no chance for his entire race. Even the trickster god couldn't be laughing now.

Voice barely audible, Marlis asked, "Is this my fault?"

Mek patted her shoulder. "Of course not. The nanites were obviously too weak by the time we inoculated you."

But the question jarred Noatak from his daze. Marlis's temperature had risen in the weapons locker. Risen during their kiss. What if *he* was responsible? He'd been careful not to ping her, to only savor the physical interaction, the feel of her body, her lips, her scent. An ionic connection would've been a much deeper thing. Something more instinctual and uncontrolled. He'd been careful, hadn't he?

He looked at her face, her porcelain skin and tawny eyes. The strong but slender line of her throat. The rise and fall of her breasts from her rapid breathing. He wanted to take her in his arms and comfort her, but he had nothing to give. He could never be the one to give her anything, not now or ever.

Throat tight, he backed toward the door. "I'll tell the captain the bad news."

Marlis blanched, squeezing her eyes closed. "I'm sorry."

"Not your fault," Mek reiterated and glanced toward Noatak. "I'm going to keep Marlis here a while longer for observation. Tell Qaiyaan to call a crew meeting. Everyone should know."

Stumbling from the med bay in a daze, Noatak headed toward Qaiyaan's cabin.

What if it's my fault?

Knocking once on Qaiyaan's cabin door, he opened it and entered before the captain could respond.

Lisa lay on the bed in her panties, reading something on her polycom. She yanked a blanket over her naked torso. "Hey!"

Qaiyaan looked up from his desk near the view port. "What the hell?"

"I just came from the med lab." Noatak took a seat across from the captain with his back toward the bed. His words felt thick. "The nanites are dead."

"No!" Lisa gasped behind him amidst the rustle of fabric.

Qaiyaan winced and closed his eyes. "Are you certain? Perhaps they just need more time."

"Mek verified it several times." Noatak swallowed, forcing down bile. "I think it's my fault."

"What are you talking about?" Qaiyaan frowned at him.

"I kissed her."

Empathy dawned on the captain's face. "A kiss isn't enough to destroy the nanites."

"It might if they were already weak." Noatak refused to be assuaged. "I took her straight to the med bay, but it was too late."

"Slow down, Noatak. We all know the nanites can cause blackouts when agitated, but the only thing strong enough to actually kill them is the denaidan mating frequency."

"Mek said they were struggling. The kiss made Marlis's immune system reject them." The more Noatak thought about it, the more he knew this had been his fault. He'd been careless, greedy for Marlis's touch even though he knew it could never amount to anything. Now not only was his race doomed, but Marlis'd been denied a chance for healing.

"*Iluq*, if the nanites were that vulnerable, Mek would've kept Marlis in the med bay, not let her run around among the crew."

Noatak wasn't listening. He had to make this right. If there was one thing he'd learned about regret, it was that looking back didn't move you forward. There was only one solution to losing the nanites. "We have to go after Doug. Now."

"We're working on that." Qaiyaan nodded. "We're just waiting for Kashatok to dig up more information."

"We've seen how long that takes. Doug could be dead before we track him down."

"Kashatok's working on it, believe me."

Noatak shook his head. He had another plan in mind. "Syndicorp still wants Lisa back, right? The scientists on the *Icarus* especially, I'd imagine."

Qaiyaan scowled at him. "We're not using her as bait."

"No, but we could use knowledge of her to draw them out."

"What are you suggesting?"

Noatak grinned. Nothing better than a dangerous mission to take the mind off one's troubles. "I'll send a message on Galactic Ops' old channel and claim to have information about Lisa, but that I'll only give it to the captain of the *Icarus* in person. I'll take our shuttle and meet them at some obscure location. Once they bring me on board, I'll drop a tracker. You'll be able to locate the *Icarus* and hijack them."

Qaiyaan crossed his arms. "They'll be on the lookout for that kind of thing. And we can't allow them to get their hands on you. You know too much."

Taking a deep breath to steady himself, Noatak said, "They won't get anything out of me. I'll use a suicide pill right after I drop the tracker."

"Are you insane?" Qaiyaan rose from his chair, staring Noatak down as if he was considering throwing him in the brig. "A suicide pill?"

Lisa had dressed and made her way to Qaiyaan's side. She looped one arm over his shoulder and pulled him back into his seat. "I appreciate you wanting to help save my brother, but Qaiyaan's right. This is too extreme."

"It's not." He swallowed. "I'm already dying, Qaiyaan."

As he explained about his ionic heart, Qaiyaan's face lost its color. Lisa covered her mouth with one hand, eyes glistening. When he'd finished, she lowered the hand and reached for his. "Are you damaged because you helped save me?"

When they'd rescued her from the Cartel, he'd extended his ionic shield to protect her during burn. The added strain on his system certainly hadn't helped his condition, but the root of the problem was his fault, not hers.

"No." He squeezed her hand and met her gaze steadily, so she'd know he was sincere. "I've known my ionic system was failing for years. Too much stim use while I was in the service. But I have enough left in me to do this. I don't want to go out like an old man. If I succeed at this, my death will at least mean something. I'll free your brother, get nanites for mates, and help Marlis heal."

"Marlis?" Lisa narrowed her eyes at him. "This is about her, isn't it?"

"This is about our entire race," Noatak said, pulling free of her grasp. "But I do want her future to be happy."

Lisa raised her brows. "I bet it won't be if you're gone."

"We hardly know each other." He swallowed, thinking of Marlis insisting she wanted to be with him. She was perfect, more than he'd ever imagined possible in a woman. But he could never be what she deserved. "She'll move on. But I should go before she grows any more attached."

Sighing, Qaiyaan dropped his chin to his chest. "I hate to admit it, but it's the best plan we've had so far." He rose. "I'll have Kashatok host a crew meeting in the *Kinship's* galley so everyone can attend. We need to tell the men about the nanites and he can provide any new information he might have about the *Icarus.*"

Chest tight, Noatak nodded. He knew his captain well; this was Qaiyaan's version of agreeing to the plan. Assuming Kashatok hadn't come up with a wild scheme of his own, Noatak would be on his way soon. Hopefully, he'd be remembered as a hero, the man who'd ensured future mates for his people. And once he was gone, Marlis could move on and bond with one of the remaining crew.

He should go to his bunk and prepare himself to meet *Ellam Cua*. Make sure his affairs were in order. Instead, he headed back to the med bay. All he wanted to do between now and his death was spend time with Marlis.

Chapter Thirteen

Marlis tamped down her anger as she left Mek behind in the med bay. The nanites were gone, along with the promise of healing her brain and any chance to be with Noatak. Fuck, her job might even be on the line. What was the crew going to do with her now that she'd basically killed their only hope of having mates? She was useless. A Weapons Specialist with memory problems who couldn't even manage to keep micro computers alive in her brain.

She stormed around the corner and smack into Noatak's chest. "Umph."

His hands grasped her shoulders, steadying her. Even without the nanites, electricity raced across her skin, tingling her erogenous zones. She looked up into his face. Deep within his eyes, she could see sadness. Yearning. It was like looking in a mirror.

She tried to smile, but it felt like a grimace. "How'd the captain take the news?"

Noatak sighed. "He's asked to hold a meeting on the *Kinship* to tell everyone. I came to get you and Mek."

Great. She'd hoped she had a little more time. Perhaps a chance to talk to Emmy before facing the rest of the crew.

Noatak took her hand and squeezed gently. "They won't blame you."

The tender gesture made her throat tighten. She nodded, wanting to believe him. He told Mek about the meeting, then led her across the boarding tube to the larger ship. The tightness in her throat moved to her chest as they entered the galley. Kashatok's crew already had a bottle of rum circulating among them, possibly suspecting what was coming, and the mood was somber as Marlis sat near one end of the table next to Emmy. Noatak calmly took the chair on her other side. How could he be so stoic? She wanted to run and scream and shoot things.

Once Mek had joined them, Qaiyaan took a chair at the head of the table and cleared his throat. "You probably suspect why we've called you here." The crew rumbled, nodding heads and frowning. "Mek has confirmed that the nanites are dead."

It was as if the room itself gasped, and Tovik asked, "What happened?"

"They were no longer viable by the time I inoculated her," Mek said, accepting the bottle of rum from Tovik and taking a swallow. "It's not Marlis's fault."

Emmy reached under the table and squeezed Marlis's hand while the men grumbled and muttered.

Marlis kept her focus on Qaiyaan, unable to look at the crew or Emmy or even Noatak. She'd let everyone down.

Qaiyaan continued, "This means we need to double our efforts to find Lisa's brother. Noatak has come up with a plan that may work. But there will be a cost." He gestured to his First Mate. "I'm going to let him explain."

A plan? Marlis should've known Noatak would come up with something. She dared a sideways look in his direction.

Noatak's face was sterner than usual as he looked around at the gathered men. "If the lab's on the *Icarus* like we think, our biggest difficulty will be finding the flagship. It's equipped with the latest cloaking technology and appears to be operating under comm silence."

Marlis frowned. Why did the *Icarus* sound familiar? She lifted her wrist and spoke in a low voice to Twerp. "Twerp, do I know that name?"

"Your sister is stationed on the SNV flagship *Icarus*," Twerp supplied, loud enough for everyone to hear.

The bottom dropped out of Marlis's stomach.

Chignik lowered the rum bottle to the table with a loud *thunk*. "*Anaq!* Did you just say your sister's on the *Icarus?*"

Everything came back to Marlis in a flood. She pressed her palm flat against her thigh to prevent herself from reaching for the comfort of her E-11. "Attie got promoted to corporal just before I left." She swallowed. Stupid memory had failed her again. She should've recognized the name during that first debrief. "She's the admiral's administrative attaché."

Noatak's face paled. "You never mentioned that."

"Can you find out where the ship's at?" Tovik asked.

"Better yet, can you get us on board?" Chignik added.

Noatak rubbed his face. "*Uminaq.* It's a corp flagship. The crew isn't allowed to reveal their location, and they're definitely not going to give us a tour just because Marlis is with us. Let's stick to my plan."

"The one where you commit suicide?" Qaiyaan crossed his arms and raised an eyebrow at his First Mate. "I'm up for alternate suggestions."

Marlis gasped, and the entire galley erupted with stunned confusion. She turned to Noatak. "What's he talking about?"

Noatak sighed and raised his chin defiantly. "I'll send a message out that I have information about Lisa. The corp wants her back, so they'll bite. Once I'm on board the *Icarus*, I'll plant a tracker, leaving you a trail to follow and hijack the ship."

"But he'll have to kill himself to keep them from interrogating him," Qaiyaan added.

The galley grew louder as men pounded the table and shoved back chairs, arguing with each other. Tovik had risen and was standing toe-to-toe with Noatak, gesturing wildly.

Noatak stood his ground. "I'm dying, anyway. Think of this as my final wish. You can thank me by naming your *terpak* kids after me."

More questions flew. "What do you mean, you're dying?"

"What the fuck, Noatak?"

Marlis's pulse raced and Twerp buzzed her wrist until her hand felt numb. She'd been through enough military strategy simulations to know this was a bad plan, and not only because it meant Noatak's death. "This plan is stupid." She turned to Qaiyaan. "You're the captain. Don't let him do this."

Qaiyaan raised an eyebrow, probably thinking about punishing her for insubordination, but she didn't care. Noatak couldn't be allowed to die. Not like this. The captain's gaze softened, and he turned away from her. "It is stupid. But it's all we have."

Twerp's usually soothing voice cut through the tension. "May I offer a suggestion?"

The crew fell silent, staring at Marlis's wrist. Twerp continued, "I have analyzed the feasibility of this plan, and determined there is a seventy-eight point eight percent chance the *Icarus* would detect a tracker and nullify it before it could broadcast a signal."

"See?" Tovik said, pointing at Twerp and glaring toward Noatak. At least he seemed to be on her side.

"If the immediate goal is to find the flagship," Twerp's usually smooth voice stuttered. "I suggest we allow Marlis to send her sister a message with a return receipt. The receipt can be encoded with a universal pin that will not provide ongoing spatial data, but it will provide the ship's location at that moment in time. There is a minimal six point five percent chance the *Icarus* would detect the true purpose of such a marker."

Chignik clapped his hands once. "*Assirpaa!* A marker within a marker! And if she keeps up a dialogue, we'll get a stream of information that might provide a heading."

"C-correct," Twerp said.

Noatak's face was dark. "A universal pin can't provide the same information as a tracker. You won't know when the ship enters and exits burn, so you won't be able to sneak up on them."

Tovik raised a hand. "I still have that cloaking device from the rakwiji ship the Cartel sent after us. It's not the latest technology, but it could work well enough to hide a shuttle."

"A shuttle? As in, two or three people?" Noatak crossed his arms and shook his head. "A team that small can't take down a flagship."

"But we might be able to get on and then off again before they notice," Marlis said, her mind racing. "And maybe I could convince Attie to leave with us. I know the layout of the *Icarus*. The carrier I grew up on is one of its sister ships."

"Are there alternate ways to get on board other than the standard hatchways?" Qaiyaan asked.

"Um," Marlis blanched, trying to remember details about the carrier. "Maybe Twerp knows?"

"Accessing." Twerp hiccuped a couple of times. "The *Icarus* is equipped with eight torpedo tubes which lead into the artillery bay. Assuming the weapons are not armed, one might be able to enter the hull plating at any of those points."

"*Assirpaa*! I'm so glad we hired you!" Tovik's face glowed.

Qaiyaan scratched his beard. "At least this plan doesn't include anyone killing themselves."

"It's still suicide!" Noatak's face had a blue-green tinge and his chest rose and fell rapidly. "You can't send Marlis."

Marlis stood slowly, glowering at Noatak. "Are you saying I'm incapable? Because you hired me for just this kind of job."

His mouth dropped open. "That's not what I mean at all."

"So it's settled." She lifted her chin and faced the rest of the crew. "Noatak and I will track down the *Icarus*."

Chapter Fourteen

The *Hardship* dropped the shuttle near Zyrinic Eight, the last known location of the *Icarus*. Noatak checked that Marlis was secure in her harness. He was still fuming about having her along. She wouldn't be safe just because she was someone's sister. And if she was in danger, he couldn't take the easy way out with a suicide pill. He needed to stay alive to protect her. *Uminaq*, this wasn't how this mission was supposed to happen.

"Stop scowling," she said. "I'd prefer not to be pissed at each other for the entire mission."

This might be a fool's errand, but at least he got some alone-time with Marlis. Small consolation, considering nothing could come of it even if they survived, but right now he'd accept any pleasure he could get.

Letting out a slow breath, he hit the thrusters. The shuttle didn't have the range of a burn drive, but Tovik's modifications had given the propulsion unit a boost, and Noatak's stomach lurched with the acceleration. He wasn't used to traveling without using his ionic power, but he couldn't risk giving himself an ionic system failure when he needed to stay alive for Marlis. The shuttle slowed as it reached its coordinates, and the stars outside the view screen realigned, revealing the pale blue disk of Zyrinic Eight's nearby moon.

He turned to Marlis. "All right. As Joy's so fond of saying; showtime."

Marlis grinned at him—why did he love that so much? Her excitement for this mission was almost infectious. Almost. He forced his face back into his usual stoic lines.

After entering her sister's messaging address, Marlis leaned toward the comm. "Hey, Attie, it's me! Just wanted to let you know I'm okay. It feels like we're jumping all over the galaxy with deliveries. No real action yet. Being a guard is kinda boring so far. I know, I know, you and Dad will both hope I never see combat. But damn, I'm itching for something more interesting than flying from colony to colony. I did meet a hot guy, though." She wiggled her eyebrows, then looked over her shoulder as if she'd heard something. "Shit, gotta go. I'll call again later."

Ending the call, she looked triumphantly at Noatak.

"What the hell was that?" he asked. The less the corp knew about his presence, the better.

"Calm down." She crinkled her nose. "Now she's sure to open the next message I send right away."

He settled back in his seat, trying not to smile. "You're more conniving than you give yourself credit for."

She grinned. "Thank you." The grin faded. "Although I'm feeling a little guilty using my sister like this."

"I understand." He nodded, appreciating how important family was to her. "If things go as planned, you won't have to worry about her anymore."

"That would be a relief." She stretched both arms over her head, drawing his gaze to her breasts, then rose and stood in the low doorway to the cockpit, the curve of her hip right at his eye level as she looked into the small passenger area. "What shall we do while we wait for her to open the message?"

He swallowed, wrenching his gaze from her perfectly round ass. All he could think about was how she would feel cupped in both hands.

Her glance over her shoulder revealed a sly smile that told him she knew exactly what he was thinking. The woman was a *tunrak* for sure, sent to tempt him by *Ellam Cua* himself. On impulse, he reached over and smacked her butt cheek.

She startled, banging her head on the overhead beam between the cockpit and the back end.

He was out of his seat in an instant. He'd smacked his head on that beam too many times to count. "You okay?"

"I'm fine. Didn't expect you to be so playful." She turned to face him, one hand against her forehead while a tiny trickle of blood streamed toward her eye. "You're taller than I am. How do you keep from knocking yourself out in here all the time?"

He laughed, despite himself. "Suffer enough bumps, you learn to be careful." He herded her to the shuttle's rear and pulled out a bunk stowed against the wall. "Sit. I'll get a med kit."

While he patched her up, he shook his head. "*Ellam Cua* has an evil sense of humor."

"Why would you say such a thing?" She winced as he secured adhesive to her forehead. "Isn't *Ellam Cua* your god?"

"He's a trickster." Balling up the used swabs and adhesive backing, he aimed for the refuse bin and tossed. The jumbled mess stuck to the lid, not heavy enough to activate the expulsion unit. He turned back to Marlis. "After I volunteered for this mission—which is still probably suicide, by the way, I hope you realize that—all I could think about was spending my last moments with you. *Ellam Cua* granted me my wish. The irony must have him in stitches."

She tilted her head. "Well, what can we do to make him laugh even more?" The seductive smile on her face even made the bandage across her forehead look sexy. "It could be awhile before we hear back from Attie."

Her innuendo made his cock surge to life. He'd never imagined wanting a woman this badly. She had a hold on him he couldn't explain. He'd do anything for her, and if she wanted to mess around, he was game. There would be no climax for him, but he would give her a hell of a good time.

Rising from his seat on the edge of the bunk, he looked

down at her, savoring every luscious curve. "I have a few ideas."

She licked her lips, one hand moving over her collarbone. Everything she did was seductive. Surely she knew the effect she had on him.

"Lean back." He moved to the bed and straddled her, both knees on the hard mattress.

She fell back onto her elbows, her gaze never leaving his.

He put one palm between her breasts and pushed gently, forcing her all the way down. Now he towered over her, cock thrumming against his pants. He couldn't take things all the way, but he was going to take as much as he could. Leaning forward with his weight on his hands, he captured her mouth, flicking his tongue greedily between her parted lips. She tasted amazing, sweet and fresh and warm. He dropped to his elbows, burying his hands into her hair and driving his tongue into her.

Her hands fisted the hem of his shirt, stretching the fabric to expose his skin. He contracted his abs, letting her pull the shirt up and over his shoulders, breaking the kiss only long enough to be free of the shirt. Once his lips claimed hers again, he slid one hand along her ribs to her hip, pausing there to slide a thumb beneath her waistband into the hollow beside her hipbone. She flexed against him, and he continued stroking along the outside of her thigh, aligning his body against hers. They would be such a perfect match. He could only imagine the exquisite warmth of her pussy around him, her legs hooked over his hips as he drove inside her with pure abandon.

But that couldn't be. He had to satiate himself on everything but that.

Using the hand still in her hair, he pulled her head gently to one side, giving him access to her throat. Nipping and suckling his way down its gentle curve, he filled himself with her fresh linen scent. He moved the hand at her hip upward, sliding beneath her shirt, palm skimming her flesh until it came to rest under the swell of her breast. *Assirpaa,* her breast. He wanted to see it, touch it, taste it.

Pulling back, he shoved her shirt upward, exposing a swath of creamy skin. A simple bra confined her ample breasts, the kind issued in the service, but he found it sexier than lace. It was pure Marlis.

While she wriggled off her shirt, he slid one hand beneath her back and unfastened the bra's clasp. Her breasts popped free, perfect globes large enough that his palm could barely cover one. Each rosy pink nipple begged to be tasted. Leaning forward, he captured one aroused tip, drawing as much of her breast into his mouth as he could and circling his tongue around the puckered areola.

She moaned and arched upward to meet him, encouraging him to take more. The nipple hardened beneath his tongue, and her hands roamed his naked sides and back. She widened her legs, allowing his cock to press against her core of heat through their clothing.

Ellam Cua. He wanted to bury himself in her. To fill her and claim her and make her his. Clenching his ass muscles, he pushed against her cloth-covered entrance, groaning at the exquisite pressure. Sliding down her body, he lapped at her skin, tasting the softness of her flesh, while his hands undid the clasp of her pants. She complied by lifting her hips as he pushed the waistband down, taking her panties with them. Now she was fully exposed to him, the downy mound of hair glistening with her arousal. "Beautiful."

She moaned as his breath brushed over her skin, breasts heaving as she panted. One of her hands slid down her abdomen and delved into her cleft, pleasuring herself in a way that nearly sent him over the edge just watching her.

Placing one hand over hers, he slid his fingers into her tight folds. She cried out, bucking upward, and his cock surged with need. She was so wet. So perfect.

Her free hand grabbed his, urging him deeper. He added a second finger and buried both digits to the top knuckles. The heated ridges of her pussy quivered against him and she gasped, her slickness intensifying. She bucked and pulsed, her own fingers still working the nub of her clit. "God, yes. Be inside me."

The scent of her arousal engulfed him. He had to be careful, or he'd become an animal. Tear off his clothes and take her without regard for the consequences.

Pulling back, he stared at her glorious sex while he plunged two, then three fingers in and out of her. Her middle finger furiously worked her clit while she watched him with hooded eyes.

"You are so sexy." His voice came out rough and breathy. His ionic instincts were pushing his boundaries, but he kept himself under control, focusing only on her pleasure. Curling his fingers to hit that spot deep inside her that would bring her to the edge.

Her pussy convulsed. The hand on her clit jerked free, clutching the mattress beside her. She threw her head back, eyes closed as a moan rose from her lips.

Lowering his head, he let his mouth take over for her fingers, laving his tongue over her swollen nub while his fingers continued driving inside her. *Ellam Cua.* She tasted even better than she smelled, her pheromones permeating his senses. He clamped his lips around her clit and sucked.

Her moan rose to a scream that was pure music to his ears as she exploded around him, drenching his hand and beard with wetness.

He slowed his pace, but refused to stop until he was sure he'd wrung every shudder from her body.

She lay there panting, her alabaster skin flushed a glorious pink. Reaching weakly for him, she whispered, "Come here. You should get yours, too."

Oh, Ellam Cua, you are cruel. The one thing he could never have with her was full satisfaction; nanites or not, it was a death sentence for one of them. He wrapped one hand around hers. "I can't, remember?"

She sagged against the mattress, her gaze suddenly pained.

Grabbing a thick square of gauze from the med kit, he dried his beard, then lowered himself beside her, wrapping her in his arms. His cock throbbed in a painful protest, but he'd grown accustomed to ignoring its demands. He brushed his lips against her ear. "It's enough I got to experience you. No matter what happens, I'll cherish that forever."

They lay together, content, until the comm beeped with an incoming message.

Marlis sat bolt upright. "Attie."

She looked down at him, and he could tell she wasn't ready for their moment to an end, either. But the mission had to take precedence. He pressed a kiss to her palm and rose. "You have to answer."

Marlis scrambled back into her clothing and they returned to the cockpit. Attie had indeed responded to the message. This was his first glimpse of her sister, and he was startled by how alike they looked as her image filled the screen. "Hey Marlis, I got your messages. I'm thrilled you found a job, but it would be good to know what ship you're on so I can calm Dad down. He's on the warpath, insisting you've been kidnapped into slave labor or something."

He unthreaded the location code from the return receipt while Marlis watched the rest of the message. She'd been right about hooking her sister with a love interest, and he tried to shut out the details of Attie's latest fling while he worked. His heartbeat sped up when he realized the flagship was close; it'd never left Zyrinic Eight's solar system.

After her sister's message ended, he said, "That message came from within this system. Unless they plan to burn out of here soon, we could be on them within the next jump."

She nodded, frowning. "I'd hoped we'd have more time."

Reaching over, he took her hand. "There will never be enough time."

CHAPTER FIFTEEN

Marlis felt torn as she recorded her next message. She never wanted her time with Noatak to end, but they were on a mission, and they had to act now, before the *Icarus* left the system. Knowing her sister would detect something wrong if she acted too chipper, Marlis half-invented a problem for her next message. "Hey, Sis. I know I just messaged you, but I wish you were here to talk to. The guy I mentioned before? He says he wants to be with me, but then keeps making excuses why he can't."

Noatak raised an eyebrow at her but didn't remark, keeping most of his attention on the console.

They were orbiting one of Zyrinic's inner planets, a gas giant surrounded by several rings. The fine particulate that made up the outer ring was wreaking havoc on their sensors, but this was near the last pinpointed location of the *Icarus*.

Just as she sent her message, Noatak leaned closer to the view screen and began furiously tapping the sensor keypad. "*Uminaq*, there they are. I need to get our cloak up."

She scanned the glowing ring of the planet and spotted the massive flagship doing a lazy rotation, ripples of particulate billowing around its sharp angles and jutting weapon turrets. Her pulse raced. If they were spotted now, the mission would be over. If the *Icarus* decided to shoot first and ask questions later, they'd be vaporized. She held her breath, waiting.

Once the cloaking system was up, Noatak raised his hands off the console and focused on the view screen. "I don't think they detected us through the particulate ring, but we'll hang out here a few minutes to be sure."

Letting out a long sigh, she let her gaze rove over the swirling orange planet's surface. "Why are they parked here? This is an uninhabitable planet."

"No idea, but they just made our mission one hell of a lot easier."

After what felt like forever, Noatak nodded. "If they knew we were here, they'd've demanded identification by now. Let's move."

With a nod, she retreated to the back of the shuttle and put on a vacuum suit. Noatak would fly the tiny shuttle along the massive flagship's underside, moving slowly enough to avoid any proximity detectors. Apparently, the pirates had done this kind of thing before.

The vacuum suit was a snug fit over her breasts, and she was struggling with the seal when a sharp jolt stung her wrist. Pausing, she looked at her wristband. "Twerp, you okay?"

Twerp let out several garbled words, out of which Marlis could only make out, "… reaction t-to certain frequenciesssss…" The sentence ended on a hiss of static.

"Twerp?" A lump filled her throat. "What's going on?"

From the cockpit, a stranger's voice came over the comm. "Unidentified vessel, please shut down all systems and prepare to be towed."

The ship shuddered, and she stumbled forward to where Noatak was frantically tapping the keypads. "What's happening?"

"They spotted us. *Uminaq*, they have us in a tractor beam."

She gripped the head rests on the cockpit chairs and tried to remain upright as the ship jolted again. "Fuck, do as they say. We haven't done anything wrong. Maybe they'll let us go."

"I'm on their most-wanted list, Marlis. There's no getting out of this for me. But you can." He grabbed her, kissing her hard, then swung her in front of himself before flicking the comm to life. "I'm holding one of your citizens hostage. Release the tractor beam or I'll kill her."

She struggled against his solid grip, more out of instinct than fear. "No!"

"We do not deal with terrorists," the man on the other end of the comm replied.

The shuttle jerked forward, driving her hard against Noatak's chest. She couldn't take a breath, and her vision closed in as the flagship seemed to draw closer at breakneck speed. A strange tingling surrounded her, almost a numb sensation.

And then the world went black.

Noatak instinctively engaged his ionic shielding and wrapped it around Marlis when the tractor beam jerked the shuttle forward with a force that had to be close to ten G's. He held on as long as he could, ionic heart ramped to an agonizing pace. The shuttle hurtled toward an open landing bay, but he blacked out before they reached it.

He woke in a tiny cell barely large enough for him to lie flat on the floor. There was no furniture, no fixtures, no panels, no door that he could see. After taking a quick assessment of himself—his chest and head hurt, but there appeared to be no other damage—he stood, scouring the corners of the bare metal walls for any sign of a camera or an access panel.

"Hello?" His voice seemed too loud in the small space.

His last memory was of clutching Marlis against him, putting all of his willpower into shielding her from the deadly force of the beam. Had she survived? *Anaq*, had *he* survived? For all he knew, this was *Ellam Cua's* perverse version of hell.

Suddenly, a section of the wall slid aside, revealing a sparkling transparent energy shield separating him from the interior of a brightly lit laboratory. Stainless steel counters, several empty exam tables, and scattered medical equipment that Mek would've salivated over filled the room. On the far wall, two other doors similar to Noatak's shone with energy fields.

A man with shiny dark hair stepped around one of the lab tables, eyeing him with a sick, appraising hunger. "In my wildest dreams, I never imagined I'd get my hands on a denaidan male." He smiled, showing straight white teeth. "Fortune must be smiling on me."

Noatak moved as close to the energy shield as he dared. "What the fuck does that mean?"

The man looked down at an oversized polycom in his hands. "Noatak qutar'Kon, a corporal in Galactic Ops, AWOL for fifteen years and wanted for acts of piracy and terrorism." He looked back up, eyes gleaming. "You're so lucky we found you. Any other ship would've executed you on the spot." Setting the polycom aside, he made a gesture and three well-armed troopers appeared from the unseen corners of the room. "My name's Dr. Dollard. We'll be spending a lot of time together."

One trooper moved toward Noatak, and the shield dropped. Noatak eyed the man, wondering if he could take him out with an ionic pulse. He was surprised to even be alive after exerting himself in the shuttle, and calling on his ionic power now might very well kill him. But he still needed to find Marlis, no matter the cost.

Dollard said, "The dampening in here makes using your ionic abilities impossible, so don't even try. Come out."

Uminaq. Of course they'd thought of that. He stepped into the lab, familiarizing himself with the layout and looking for any potential weapons. "The woman I was with—my hostage. She survive?"

The doctor was aligning surgical tools neatly on a tray next to a stainless steel exam table. "The tractor beam should've turned you both to pulp. Our captain was quite surprised to find you both alive." Dollard met his gaze with a smirk. "It's also how I knew we'd captured a denaidan."

It was all Noatak could do not to sag to his knees with relief. Marlis was alive.

Adjusting the exam table so it stood on end, Dollard gestured toward it. "If you please."

Several straps dangled from the table's edges. *Restraints.* So he was to be tortured. One of the troopers nudged Noatak in the lower back, forcing him forward. Noatak tried to keep his voice even. "What are you planning to do?"

"Denaidan ionic powers have always fascinated me, especially the different way each gender uses the ability. Your males are so brutish with their ionic strength, while your females excel at empathic connections that are nearly impossible to test empirically."

"You fucking killed all our females," Noatak snarled. "How would you know?"

"Mmm." The man picked up a stim-gun. "I recommend you cooperate if you want to live.

"Keep that thing away from me." Noatak stepped back, but the men on either side of him caught his arms and dragged him forward, cinching him down.

Dollard jabbed a stim-gun into Noatak's arm.

The adrenaline already coursing through Noatak's veins ignited. He yelled and jerked hard against the straps.

Non-plussed, Dollard gave him several more inoculations before waving a scanner over Noatak's chest, face pinched into a frown. "Hmm. It appears you've sustained some ionic system damage over the years."

"Only because of people like you," Noatak spat. His mouth felt full of cotton, and spittle drooled from the corners.

"Unfortunate." The doctor stepped back, wiping a fleck from the back of his hand. "This is a significant flaw in my data set. Regardless, it will be interesting to see how the nanites perform in an ionic system like yours."

Turning, Dollard headed for the exit, his goons close behind, leaving Noatak alone in the lab.

Breath ragged, Noatak jerked against the straps over and over, all the while thinking, *Holy Ellam Cua, I've just been injected with nanites.*

CHAPTER SIXTEEN

Marlis woke to the inside of a med bay. Bright lights shone directly overhead, adding daggers to her already splitting headache. She tried to roll over to escape the glare, but couldn't move. Her arms and legs were strapped to a cot. Panic seized her, and she thrashed against the bindings.

An unfamiliar man in a crisp blue Syndicorp doctor's uniform filled her vision, blocking the overhead lights. "Calm down, Miss Swan."

All she could think was that she was in lockdown again. *What did I do?* "You can release me now."

He backed away, allowing a familiar face to appear. "Attie?" Marlis held back the catch in her voice. She still didn't remember why she was here, but she knew panic would only make things worse. *There is no danger.* "Please tell him to unstrap me."

Attie looked over her shoulder. "Are the straps necessary?"

The restraints loosened. Forcing herself to remain sedate, she sat up, looking around the unfamiliar med bay. "Where am I?"

"You don't remember what happened?" Attie asked.

Marlis touched the bandage covering a sore bump on her forehead as memories slowly returned. *Noatak. The shuttle. The Resistance.* Her pulse spiked again. She must've been captured. Where was Noatak? And why wasn't Twerp buzzing? She reached for her wrist and found the band gone. "Twerp? Where's Twerp?"

Attie shook her head. "Our tech team had to confiscate your AI. They'll give it back once they've pulled the information and made sure it's not bugged."

Marlis nearly choked. What kind of information about the Resistance might Twerp reveal? Her voice sounded tinny and fake as she calmly asked, "Why would you think I'm bugged?"

"You're traveling with a known criminal," a man's voice came from the door across the large bay. Marlis turned to find a small man wearing a black admiral's uniform approaching, followed by three well-armed troopers. He seemed rather young to be an admiral, with a head of brown hair untouched by gray. "A pirate who would do anything to get his hands on Syndicorp technology."

"Noatak?" The name left her lips before she could reign herself in. Noatak'd told her he was a wanted man. That's why his original plan had included suicide. Oh God, had he committed suicide? She shot to her feet and looked around the med bay, hoping to see his familiar copper skin. The only other patient was a woman in a bed at the far end of the room. "Where is he?"

Attie put a hand on her shoulder. "Don't worry. The pirates can't hurt you now."

More memories crashed over Marlis. The crew of the *Icarus* must think she'd been a hostage. Noatak'd set this all up to make her appear innocent. Fuck, had they executed him? She needed to know if he was alive.

"Corporal Swan," the admiral addressed Attie. "You have confirmed this is your sister?"

Attie stiffened, her hand moving up in salute. "Yes, sir."

With a stiff nod, he focused his icy-blue gaze on Marlis. "My name is Admiral Olly, standing officer of the SNV *Icarus*, with full authority under Syndicorp law to carry out immediate punishment to traitors of the regime."

Marlis swallowed, her breath coming in short gasps. Noatak was probably dead. She couldn't make her eyes focus, so she concentrated on her breathing. *In. Out. In. Out.* She longed for Twerp's familiar buzz.

The admiral continued, "Marlis Swan, you stand accused of associating with known pirates and conspiring to engage in illegal activities against Syndicorp and its allies."

"Sir—" Attie began, but was cut off by the admiral raising one hand.

"You will remain silent, Corporal. Your part in this has yet to be determined."

Fuck. Not only was Noatak dead, she'd put Attie in danger. None of this mission was going according to plan. She reached instinctively for her weapon.

The troopers behind the admiral pointed their rifles at her just as she realized her holster was empty. *Fuck, they disarmed me!*

Attie gently squeezed Marlis's arm. "Take a breath, Marlis. There is no danger." Her sister moved part way between Marlis and the armed guards. "Sir, please forgive her. She suffers from PTSD."

"I've read her file," the admiral continued, gaze still cold. "I understand she was turned down for active duty due to mental health issues. However, I will not accept that as an excuse. You are facing a charge of treason. How do you plead?"

Treason? She could barely breathe, barely think. She had to get a grip on herself if she hoped to get her and Attie through this alive. What would Attie do? She met her sister's steady blue gaze, but behind her eyes, Marlis detected a reflection of her own panic. Her sister had always been her rock. Now Marlis needed to do whatever it took to save Attie.

She turned back to the admiral. If he believed Marlis had mental health issues, she could play the victim. The thought sickened her. She'd never used her condition as an excuse for anything, never wanted to be considered an imbecile, but right now, it was all she had. Thankfully, Noatak'd given her a plausible cover. She shoved aside the thought that it had been his final act. Hopefully, she'd have time to grieve later.

Fluttering both hands, Marlis said, "I'm sorry, sir. I'm just so confused and frightened right now." Thinking of

Noatak, she let tears prick her eyes. "I didn't know he was a pirate until… until…"

Admiral Olly seemed unaffected. "Tell me why you're here, and I may mitigate your sentence."

"I was hired as a guard on a cargo ship. That's all I know."

"What's your cargo?"

"I never asked, sir." She screwed her face into what she hoped was a look of terror. "Please. I need Twerp. She's the only thing that keeps me calm."

"Twerp?" He narrowed his eyes.

Attie answered, "That's what she calls her service AI."

A muscle in the admiral's jaw bulged. "Our tech team has been unable to revive your AI. It appears the pirates planted a self-destruct in its code, which was activated by our tractor beam."

Marlis gasped, legs growing weak. "Twerp's dead?"

Attie's hand on her arm tightened, and she gasped. "Oh, no."

Her chest couldn't contain any more heartache. *Not Twerp, too.* Marlis refused to believe it. Yet Twerp's last words to her had ended in static. Noatak and Twerp, both gone in a flash. Grief threatened to shut down all her logic, and she sank, trembling, backward onto the cot.

Admiral Olly took a step forward. "Tell me why you were sending messages to Corporal Swan."

Shit. Her heart threatened to explode. Attie might be punished for this entire mess. Marlis looked up into the admiral's face, her vision a tunnel she could barely see the end of. "She's my sister, sir. Don't you ever call your sister?"

"Don't try to be smart with me, Miss Swan." The admiral crossed his arms. "Your shuttle emerged from a burn cycle in this exact location around an uninhabited planet. No cargo on board, no reason to be here, and we've traced a hidden tracker embedded in your messages. What is your mission?"

She couldn't think of an excuse. At least the tears blurring her sight were real. She blinked, forcing one to flow down her cheek. "I'm just a guard," she choked out. "I don't even know how to pilot a shuttle. Noatak seduced me. I thought he was special and wanted him to meet my sister. That's all."

He turned to Attie. "This is getting us nowhere."

Attie frowned. "Sir, my sister's highly susceptible to manipulation, and this pirate obviously capitalized on that. Her messages went on and on about her new boyfriend. You saw in her file that our father applied for an extended dependency waiver, but it wasn't approved before she ran away. Whatever those pirates did to her has obviously exacerbated her PTSD."

Highly susceptible? Ran away? Marlis took a shaky breath. Attie knew she hadn't run away, and she sure as hell didn't think Marlis was easily manipulated. So Attie must be lying to help her. Of all the people in the universe, she could trust Attie. *There is no danger.* Marlis reached for her sister's hand. Much as it grated on her, she needed to keep playing the imbecile card. And Attie's life depended on Marlis's innocence.

"Sir, when can I have my AI back?" She knew she'd already asked, but asking again was one way to make him believe she was slow.

Olly made a derisive noise in the back of his throat and looked at Attie. "Is she serious?"

"Sir, you read her file." Attie squeezed Marlis's hand. "Even if she could answer your questions, the information she provided would be suspect. This is exactly why we applied for a dependency waiver. She shouldn't be roaming the galaxy on her own."

The admiral slowly shook his head, his shrewd eyes never leaving Marlis's face. Marlis blinked another tear free. After a few moments, he turned away. "Corporal Swan, I will consider leniency, but only because of your exemplary service record and the sacrifice your family has already endured. Please take your sister to your quarters and report back to my offices for further questioning. We'll transfer her to a proper medical institution at the next space station."

"Thank you, sir." Attie saluted the admiral's retreating back, waiting until he'd cleared the doorframe before looking at Marlis. "C'mon, we'd better let Dad know you're all right."

Grateful for a reprieve, Marlis followed her sister out of the med bay.

CHAPTER SEVENTEEN

Noatak jerked on his bindings again, wrists and ankles slick with blood. Each breath burned his chest and throat as if he might burst into flames at any moment. Why had he allowed Mek to talk him out of implanting a suicide pill? *Because of Marlis.* Everything he did was because of Marlis. He'd wanted to live as long as he could just for the chance to see her every day.

Ellam Cua. He loved her. That was now painfully clear. They hadn't consummated, hadn't physically bonded, but he loved her. Of that, he was certain.

Something green flashed behind the energy shield on one of the other cells, and after a moment, he realized he wasn't alone.

"Hey!" he croaked out at what must be another prisoner.

The green light moved again. A cybernetic eye?

"Hey," he called louder. "How long have you been here?"

Still nothing.

"Can you hear me?"

The door's energy field went down, allowing the occupant to step into the room. A human—or sort-of-human. Besides a cybernetic eye, one full side of the man's face was a dull gray metal. His loose clothing couldn't hide what looked like a robotic hand at the end of his sleeve.

"You're denaidan," the man said in a monotone. "Is Lisa Moss with you?"

All the breath left Noatak. "Are you Doug?"

The man nodded once, green gaze rolling over Noatak's bound body.

Noatak'd expected Lisa's twin brother to be small and wiry like her. This man was nearly as tall and broad as Noatak himself. And he was a cyborg. Was this what the nanites eventually did to a person? "Lisa sent me to save you. Unfasten me and let's get out of here."

Doug shook his head. "I cannot be saved."

Noatak eyed the man. "How did you get out of your cell? Aren't you a prisoner?"

"I am what they expect me to be."

Noatak yanked against his bindings. "Unstrap me. I have to save Marlis."

"Accessing." Doug's cybernetic eye flashed. "Marlis Swan. Sibling to—" Without warning, Doug stopped speaking and stepped backward into his cell. The energy shield flashed back to life, obscuring his form once more.

"What the hell?" Was Doug experiencing a cyborg glitch or something?

A heartbeat later, the lab's main door slid open and Dr. Dollard stepped inside, accompanied by a small man in a black uniform. Doug must've somehow sensed them coming. The small man stepped ahead of the guards and Noatak spotted the silver insignia on his crisp lapels. He was looking at the admiral himself.

"Doctor," The admiral stood facing Noatak, hands clasped behind his back while he raked his gaze down Noatak's shackled body. Noatak knew his type; the kind of man who saw the surrounding universe in a dogged contrast of black and white. "This man is one of Syndicorp's most wanted criminals for conspiracy, murder, and an entire host of treasonous activities. The CEOs will want to make an example of him."

"He's too valuable to summarily execute." Dr. Dollard edged between Noatak and the admiral. "Only a handful of his kind are left in the universe. Studying him will provide immeasurable benefits to my program."

The admiral shook his head. "I'm already considering an exception for the woman. She's obviously incapable of knowingly taking part in his criminal activities."

"It doesn't matter if the woman is guilty or not. The CEOs only need a scapegoat. Use her."

Marlis as a scapegoat? It was all Noatak could do to keep his mouth shut and listen instead of roar with frustration.

The admiral crossed his arms. "The only example she'd make is that we need to do a better job of institutionalizing our mentally ill. Her family has agreed to lock her up. I cannot make an exception for him."

Noatak's pulse raged in his ears. Marlis as a scapegoat. Marlis institutionalized. Marlis punished for crimes she never committed. And he was helpless to do a thing to stop it. He twisted his wrists against their bindings. If only he could draw on his powers; it'd be worth burning himself out to crush these men like bugs.

Dr. Dollard had picked up the polycom and thrust it under the admiral's nose. "Need I remind you that without an operational cyber-sensitive program, your ship no longer has a purpose?"

A sneer crossed the admiral's upper lip, and he focused again on Noatak. Noatak glared back, his muscles close to bursting as he strained against the straps.

"You have him until we reach Aleigh." The admiral turned away. "Then the matter's no longer in my hands." He stalked from the lab without a backward glance, his troopers trailing a few steps behind him.

Hands on his hips, Dr. Dollard watched until the door slid shut behind the men. "Bah." He plucked up a scanner and pressed it directly over Noatak's breastbone. "I suppose I'd better make the best use of our time. How are you feeling?"

Noatak glared back. He was feeling stronger, actually, probably in response to the adrenaline coursing through him.

"It's refreshing to have a purely biological subject." Dr. Dollard set the scanner aside and picked up a syringe. "Lately, I've been feeling more like a mechanic than a doctor."

The sting of the needle made Noatak's skin quiver. "What the hell are you trying to accomplish, anyway?"

The doctor seemed all-too-happy to discuss his work. "The nanites are designed to increase cybernetic awareness in humans. We call it cyber-sensitivity." He removed the syringe and moved out of Noatak's line of sight. "They create a network within the body that operates along the same lines as the denaidan ionic system—in truth, your species was the catalyst for multiple projects. My work focuses on computer frequencies rather than kinetic or empathic frequencies, but human physiology is lacking. The only way I've been able to keep test subjects alive is by incorporating robotics." Still out of visual range, Dollard rattled what sounded like glassware. "Such a shame there are so few of your species left to study."

"You mother-fucker," Noatak said through clenched teeth, knowing he should just remain silent and let the doctor carry on, but unable to repress his fury. "You committed genocide and all you care about is your experiment."

Dr. Dollard appeared at the edge of his vision again, eyes trained on his polycom. "I had nothing to do with the project that decimated your planet. But there's no sense wasting a splendid opportunity for study, especially since I only have a few days before I must hand you over to our idiotic CEOs." Using one finger, the doctor scrolled across the polycom's screen. "As I'd hoped, the nanites are replicating nicely. They seem to have an affinity for your ionic system." He looked up. "Did you know your condition was terminal?"

If Noatak'd still been foaming at the mouth, he would've spit at the doctor. As it was, he only growled low in his chest.

Dollard tapped an index finger against Noatak's breastbone. "Note I said 'was'. The nanites appear to be repairing your ionic system. It's impressive, actually. There may be applications I haven't considered." A slimy smile lifted the corners of the man's mouth. "I may be able to convince the powers-that-be to let you live."

Turning, the doctor practically skipped from the room, leaving Noatak reeling at his last words. The nanites were repairing him? Fuck. So he might live, only to rot in a cell while Marlis was dragged off to an institution.

"*Ellam Cua*, you're a mother-fucker," he muttered, shaking his head.

Chapter Eighteen

Attie all but dragged Marlis through the ship's corridors, passing curious personnel with only a brisk nod. Two trooper guards followed close behind and took positions outside the door once they reached Attie's quarters. Inside the room, her sister immediately thrust her into the small shower cubicle, clothing and all. "You must want to clean up after that pirate rubbed himself all over you," she said a little too loudly. Turning the water on full, she pointed a finger straight between Marlis's eyes. "You never cry," she whispered angrily. "What's going on?"

Mind in turmoil, Marlis balled her hands into fists and stepped sideways to avoid the bulk of the stinging flow. "Syndicorp," she started, then changed her mind. "Mom died." She wasn't making sense. "I've joined the Resistance."

Sighing, Attie adjusted the nozzle toward the wall. "We can only keep the water running a few more minutes. My room's probably being monitored, and I have to report to the admiral. Start by telling me why you're here."

Marlis blew out a controlled breath. "We're here to rescue one of the nanite test subjects."

Attie's brows drew together. "What test subjects?"

"This ship is housing a nanite test lab. The guy's name is Doug." Marlis nodded, pleased she'd remembered that detail. Water had funneled down into her boots, making her feet squishy.

"You've been misinformed." Attie crossed her arms, steam swirling around her. "We're testing a prototype sensor."

Marlis took her sister by the shoulders, looking intensely into her eyes through the steamy air. "There's a lab on this ship and whatever Syndicorp's telling you is a lie to cover up their real motives. Just like they covered up Pulati. Attie, the corp staged the terrorist attacks. Troopers killed Mom."

Attie shrugged her off. "Those pirates must have you brainwashed."

"No, I got my memories back," Marlis said. "And he's not a pirate. He's part of the Resistance."

"You do not have your memory back, Marlis. I can tell." The shower's water timer chimed that its allotment was almost up, and Attie glanced nervously over her shoulder toward her cabin.

"I didn't say ability to remember," Marlis whispered. "I said memories. Look up the documentary on RealTime News for the truth."

Attie scrunched up her face doubtfully. Speaking louder than she needed to, she said, "Are you almost done with the shower, Marlis?"

Swallowing, Marlis answered back, "Almost." Then she dropped her voice to a whisper again. "What happened to the man who was with me? Is he alive?"

"He was alive when you arrived. They're probably questioning him, but I don't have access to more information." Attie rubbed her forehead. "You know Syndicorp executes pirates and anyone who knowingly aids pirates."

Marlis's throat tightened, making it difficult to speak. Noatak could be alive! But he was going to be executed. Hell, she and Attie might be facing the same charges. "I'm sorry. I never meant to get you in trouble."

"I know." Attie cupped both hands over Marlis's cheeks, eyes suddenly brimming with tears. "I'm just glad you're alive. That tractor beam was supposed to kill you."

The shower turned itself off, and Attie stepped back, grabbing a towel from a nearby shelf and speaking loudly. "I have some fresh clothes you can borrow. I'll help you make a call to Dad, then I need to report."

The last thing on Marlis's mind was calling her father. All she wanted to know was whether or not Noatak was all right. Where could he be? Were they torturing him for information? She bit her lip, thinking of the suicide pill in his first plan. What if he'd brought one along? Her chest hurt just thinking about it, and her pounding pulse made it difficult to think straight. God, she missed Twerp.

Attie laid a civilian tunic and pants on the end of the bed. Marlis peeled out of her soaking clothes and hung them inside the shower to drip dry. Her boots were standard issue, designed to dry fast, so she set them aside and pulled on the tunic, cinching a cloth belt around her waist. "What'd they do with my pistol?"

Attie shook her head, one eyebrow raised. "Really? You think they'd give that back?"

Fuck, of course not. Losing her favorite weapon pissed her off almost as much as anything else about this situation. She hadn't felt this trapped since being confined to lockdown several years ago. She glanced around the room, looking for anything that might be used as a weapon. Everything here reminded her of her childhood. A holo-cube rotating through family photos. A standard issue blanket on the neatly made bed, turned down just enough to display the satin edged blanket underneath. A poster with a scene from a movie where two women had saved an entire planet from extinction.

"Hey!" Marlis pointed at the poster. "You stole that from our room!"

"You left it behind." Attie smirked before sobering. "And it reminded me of you."

Marlis took her sister's hands. "I wish I could do something to make the admiral understand you're innocent."

Attie took a deep breath. "He didn't throw you in the brig, so I think he's willing to believe you." She pulled her hands free and patted Marlis on the shoulder. "I hate to say it, but you'll probably be sent to some sort of assisted living facility after this. Maybe that's best, though. This whole pirate conspiracy mess is exactly the kind of thing Dad was afraid of happening if you went out on your own."

Her sister's words were like a punch in the gut. Attie had always stood up for her. Encouraged her. Even when Marlis had been in the wrong. If Attie gave up on her, Marlis had no one left. "Please don't give up on me."

Attie sighed and headed toward the door. "Get some rest. I'll be back before you know it."

With a nod to the guards outside, Attie was gone, the door sliding shut as solidly as any cell in the brig. But this might be Marlis's only chance to escape and help Noatak. Desperate, she opened Attie's closet and pawed through her things, hoping for a weapon. But Attie'd never been into guns, preferring the subtle skill of subterfuge. *Fuck!*

Pacing the room, her eyes fell once more on the poster. One frayed corner covered a maintenance panel. As a child, she'd often hidden in the conduit behind just such a panel in their bedroom during her panic attacks. The conduit ran throughout most of the ship, providing maintenance access to pipes and venting, and she'd explored the twisted avenues for potential escape routes.

What if I could use it to find Noatak?

She glanced around the corners of the room, wondering if there were cameras watching or only microphones. Would Attie be punished if Marlis escaped? If there was one thing Attie'd always been good at, it was talking herself out of trouble. Marlis had to trust Attie could this time, too. Noatak's life was on the line, and she was his only hope.

Grabbing one of Attie's spare uniforms, she put it on. She'd have to come out of the maintenance corridor at some point, and if she surfaced in civilian clothes, she might be noticed. The white corporal insignia would allow her to walk around most of the ship without being questioned. She pried the panel loose, exposing the dark, narrow space between the walls thick with piping and wires. Damn. She remembered it being a little wider.

On impulse, she raced back to the bath compartment to retrieve one of Attie's eyeliner pencils. On the back of the poster, she scrawled, *Remember what I told you,* and a heart with her initial inside, like she had when they were kids. Hopefully, Attie'd see it. Someday, Marlis planned to come back for her.

Taking a deep breath, she squeezed inside. Her back against one wall, her boobs pressed against the pipes, she took a shallow breath of dusty air and began edging down the narrow corridor.

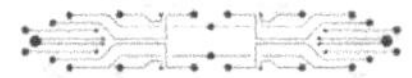

Alone in the lab once more, Noatak stared toward the cell where Doug remained hidden. Would he come out again now that Dollard was gone? Right now, Doug was his only chance of escape, and the guy seemed in no hurry to get off this ship himself.

After a few moments, the shield disappeared. Doug stood stiffly, head tilted as if he was listening to something far away, then moved into the main lab area.

"I have determined you are a potential threat to my sister if you are questioned. Therefore, I have determined I must either kill you or assist your escape."

"What the fuck?" Noatak yanked against his restraints. "We're here to rescue you, you asshole!"

"I have decided to help you escape." Doug lifted his robotic hand and severed the binding on Noatak's right wrist.

"About fucking time." Although Noatak felt like punching the cyborg right in the non-robotic eye, he reached to unfasten the binding on his other wrist while Doug cut the straps around his ankles. "Do you know how to locate Marlis?"

"She was taken to her sibling's quarters, and I disabled the monitoring devices. However, she is no longer in that location. Your companion is traveling through the maintenance corridor. It is probable she is attempting to reach the brig."

"*Uminaq,* she thinks that's where I'm being held. How far is she from here?"

"Four levels down. If she is captured, she will reveal information about Lisa. The most expedient way to ensure my sister's safety is to ignite a pressure valve at the next junction."

"What will that do?" Noatak didn't like the calculating look in the cyborg's eye.

"The flame retardant system will engage, causing asphyxiation within moments."

Noatak had Doug pinned to the wall before he even knew what he was doing. "If you even think about harming Marlis, I'll make you pay."

Doug remained emotionless. "I have dismissed the dampening field surrounding this room, but I would still recommend against using your powers."

"I'll crush you with my bare hands if I have to," Noatak said, meaning every word. "Now tell me how to get to Marlis."

"Without a means to contact her prior to her emergence in the secure area, she will be captured. I cannot allow that to happen."

"You seem to have access to this ship's systems. Marlis has an AI. Could you send a message through that?"

Once more, Doug tilted his head as if listening. "Her AI is no longer with her."

Powers or no powers, Noatak was so pumped on stims and adrenaline, he imagined he could push Doug straight through the bulkhead. "There has to be something you can do. Create a diversion or something until we can reach her."

What might've been the ghost of understanding flickered across Doug's face. "You denaidans are very dedicated to your mates."

There was no sense denying what Noatak knew to be true. Marlis was his mate, one way or another, in this life or the next. "I would die for her."

Doug's human eye blinked several times. "That may be the outcome if you attempt to help her."

Noatak relaxed the pressure of his arm against Doug's throat. "I'll risk it."

The cyborg stepped away from the wall. "Follow me."

The door slid open, revealing the blank wall of a dimly lit hallway. Turning left, they walked several paces down until Doug stopped in front of a maintenance panel. Inserting his robotic fingers into the crack, he released the panel with a pop. On the wall of the narrow corridor inside, a thick cable extended vertically in both directions, disappearing into darkness. "This conduit carries a high voltage line. It will lead to an intersection where you may intercept your mate. However, it will require the use of your ionic shield to prevent your immediate death."

"Let's go," Noatak said without hesitation. He'd burn out for Marlis if that's what it took.

Doug stepped back. "I do not possess ionic shielding. I cannot accompany you. Once you reunite with your mate, descend two more levels to the docking bays. I will assist you in any way I can from here."

"What about you?"

"I will return to my cell where I belong."

Noatak frowned. "We came here to save you."

"Please tell my sister to stop. I cannot be saved." Doug gestured to the conduit. "You must move quickly. The doctor will return soon. I will put the panel back in place behind you."

Noatak took a hard breath, steadying his nerves. He hadn't used his ionic abilities for anything major in a long time. Summoning all his reserves, he surrounded himself with his power. He wasn't sure if the tightness in his chest was his regular heart or his ionic one.

With a last glance toward Doug, he asked, "What happens if my shield fails and I die?"

Doug had picked up the panel and stood, waiting to put it back in place. "I will be forced to enact my original plan to protect my sister."

For a moment, Noatak wondered if he was being coerced into an elaborate trap. But if Doug'd wanted to kill him, he could've easily done it while Noatak had been strapped down. Grabbing ahold of the high voltage line, he squeezed into the corridor and began the journey down.

CHAPTER NINETEEN

Marlis reached the end of her first conduit and peered through the vent into the empty hallway outside. Her heart had never beaten so hard in her life. Shimmying out of the cramped tunnel, she jammed the vent panel back in place, straightened her uniform, and strode purposefully down toward the elevator. The conduits weren't connected between levels except for the high voltage intersections, so she had to take the elevator to reach the weapons locker.

That was the first order of business—arm herself. Since the ship wasn't in active combat, there was a good chance she'd be able to slip into the weapons locker unnoticed. Once armed, she'd have a much better chance of success when she reached the brig.

The elevator door slid open, allowing a colonel to exit. He frowned at her dusty uniform as he passed. Keeping her face impassive, Marlis saluted and stepped onto the elevator. Thankfully, he didn't say anything before the door slid shut.

She let out a sigh and pressed the button down. The weapons locker was sectioned off in a secure area, but she could get past the security checkpoint by using the conduit. At least, she'd been able to as a child. Stepping off the elevator, she glanced left and right, confirming she was alone before heading to the next panel.

She squeezed herself inside and did her best to pull the panel back into place behind her. The farther she got from Attie's quarters, the more she doubted her choice. Even armed, a lone woman stood little chance against the security guarding the brig. *You're not just a lone woman*, she reminded herself. *You're a marksman*. She only needed a weapon.

Verifying that the weapons locker wasn't occupied, she pushed the panel off and stepped out into the familiar neat rows of service rifles and pulse pistols. Hopefully, neither of the guards on the other side of the locker would decide to patrol in here until she was long gone. Brushing her fingers over the scope of an MCS6, she forced herself not to dawdle and grabbed a pair of standard-issue E-11 pulse pistols. Tucking one into each side of her belt, she retreated back into the maintenance conduit, securing the panel behind her.

Feeling much better now that she was armed, she moved down the conduit toward the next elevator. As she pressed her face against another vent to get her bearings, she heard a shuffling noise from the conduit ahead. Hardly daring to breathe, she peered into the darkness along the pipes. Someone was in here.

"Fuck," she said on a breath and reached for a pistol.

"Marlis?" the whisper sounded like a hiss of steam.

"Noatak?" She crept forward, one hand out in the darkness. Her palm met a broad, solid arm, and a familiar clean metallic scent reached her. She could hardly contain herself. "You're alive!"

"Shh." His hand found hers and he began leading her back the way he'd come.

He stopped where the maintenance corridor widened at the high voltage intersection, turning to face her, form lit by the tiny orange glow of a lightning-bolt danger sign. His eyes glittered in the dim light, and she slid both hands up his chest, seeking to reassure herself he was really here. He was solid and real and warm.

His arms encircled her, cheek pressed against the top of her head. How had they managed to find each other like this? She'd never believed in a god, but perhaps his *Ellam Cua* was looking out for them after all.

For a few breaths, they both stood there, neither willing to let the other go. Then he gently pushed her away. She clawed her fingers into the fabric of his shirt, not done with the moment. He smiled, then cupped her cheeks with both hands, brushing her lips with a kiss before shifting his mouth toward her ear. "I'm going to have to carry you."

Carry me? What did he mean? He turned and offered his back. Although the corridor was wider here, it was still cramped. What was he thinking? Uncertain but trusting, she looped both hands over his shoulders. He pulled her legs up over his hips and moved into the alcove holding the high voltage line. She gasped. He was going to take them down the high voltage line. *Oh, fuck!*

Next thing she knew, he was descending the cable like a monkey, with her clinging to his back for dear life. She could feel his chest heaving from the effort. How was he doing this? It had to have something to do with his ionic powers. Damn him if he killed himself trying to save her.

After what seemed like forever, he stepped out into another maintenance corridor. She released her hold and slid down his back to the floor. He leaned against the wall, the light from the tiny voltage warning sign glinting off his sweat-sheened copper skin.

Reaching out, she gripped his hand and whispered, "Are you all right?"

He'd said if he used his ionic system, he'd die. But his return grip was strong, and after a moment of rest, he nodded and whispered, "Keep moving."

Heaving a sigh of relief, she led the way out of the alcove. The conduit only went one direction from here and she squeezed between the pipes, wondering how Noatak was managing with his broad chest. But other than a few quiet exhales as he forced himself through a particularly narrow spot, he kept close behind her. At the next vent, she paused to peek outside.

The wide-open expanse of one of the docking bays stretched out before her. The *Icarus's* troop mobilization carrier took up one entire side of the bay, while several smaller ships sat on the other side, including a few fighter-ships and a scientific research vessel covered with sensor panels. Men and women moved between the ships carrying tools and equipment.

She stepped aside and pulled Noatak's ear close. "Can you fly any of those?"

He stooped to peer through the vent. After a moment, he turned to her. "Our best bet is one of the fighters."

She pulled one of the E-11's from her belt and pressed it into his hand. "You might need this."

His breath brushed her cheek as he exhaled, then his free hand was pulling her close. His mouth met hers, beard rough against her chin, and she parted her lips, tangling her tongue with his. Whether they made it or not, her time with him had been the most amazing of her life.

He pulled away, a grin glinting in the scant light coming through the vent. "Let's go."

Then he kicked the panel free.

Noatak burst from the conduit with his pistol up and ready. He damned well hoped Doug was ready, because unless someone opened the bulkhead doors, it wouldn't matter if they reached the fighter or not.

As the panel he'd kicked free clattered to the deck, a woman in coveralls spun to face him. Her eyes went wide and mouth fell open. The spanner she was holding slipped from her fingers. He took aim with the pistol Marlis'd given him, but before he could fire, the woman turned and fled, shouting an alarm.

Noatak pelted toward the fighter, Marlis close at his heels. Shouts echoed through the bay as the alarm spread. Gathering his ionic force, he shoved a boarding scaffold against the side of the ship. He didn't know how much power he had left in him, especially after that harrowing climb down the voltage cable, but he'd use whatever he had left to get Marlis to safety. "Get in!"

A pulse shot echoed off a nearby crate. Marlis halted at the base of the scaffold, firing a round toward their attackers. "You get the ship ready. I'll hold them off."

Though he wanted to protect her, his ops training told him this was the right tactical choice. Marlis could hold her own. He bounded up the scaffold and jumped into the pilot seat. The fighter's cockpit was small, made for only two people, but its speed more than made up for its small size. If they managed to clear the docking bay and avoid the *Icarus's* guns, they'd be out of range before the flagship could follow.

He skimmed through the systems check and flipped the thrusters' ignition sequence. Thank *Ellam Cua* the corp kept these vessels fueled and ready. He glanced up at the bulkhead, hoping to see the doors opening, but they remained firmly sealed. Uncertain if Doug was even listening, he said, "If you're going to help, now's the time."

Marlis had moved up the scaffold behind him and now crouched on the top outside the cockpit, returning fire against their attackers. A set of double doors across the way slid open, releasing a squad of heavily armed troopers. "*Anaq!*" He couldn't engage the shields until the canopy was sealed. "Marlis, get in!"

She fired two more shots, then tumbled into the gunner's seat. He engaged the overhead canopy, cursing at its slow descent. Pushing the wheels into gear before the canopy had sealed around them, he started the fighter toward the runway. Behind them, the ground troop was setting up a heat-seeking missile unit. If one of those projectiles hit the fighter, they were done for. Small weapons fire peppered the air, plinking against the ship's hull plating and causing alarms to sound throughout the cockpit.

Behind him, Marlis shouted, "Engaging weapons."

Ahead, the bulkhead door had opened a crack, revealing a slice of star-studded sky. Warning lights on his guidance console flashed red as he switched the ship to manual takeoff and urged the vessel forward beyond regulation limits.

The electric whine of the fighter's pulse cannon met his ears and light blossomed behind them. "Got 'em!" Marlis shouted.

Ahead, a truck pulled onto the runway, coming to a halt straight in their path. The driver jumped out and fled. Beyond, the bulkhead doors were now halfway open, enough for a fighter to pass through, but it would take all his skill.

Swearing again, he tapped the lift controls and pulled on the yoke. If he adjusted too much, he'd slam into the upper bulkhead. Too little, and they'd smash into the truck. The fighter wobbled. Rose. Its wheels bumped the truck cab as they passed over.

Then the bulkhead doors flashed by and they were exiting the bay into open space.

Chapter Twenty

Marlis kept her eye on their rear until the flagship disappeared among a million stars. She had no idea how Noatak'd done it, but he'd gotten them out of range. "Looks like we're clear."

Noatak adjusted a few more controls, then craned his neck to look over his shoulder at her. "You all in one piece?"

She nodded, thinking of how he'd used his ionic powers. "Yeah, you?"

"Doing surprisingly well."

The relief she felt couldn't outweigh her sense of failure, however. She loosened her acceleration straps and leaned forward to press her forehead against the back of his headrest. "What happens now? We didn't accomplish the mission. And I'm worried about what's going to happen to my sister."

"Did she help you escape?"

"No, I slipped away while she was being interrogated. I tried to tell her the truth about Syndicorp, but she didn't want to believe me."

"I guess we're two for two, then." He craned his neck to look at her behind him. "I met Doug."

She sat up straight. "You found him? Why didn't he come with you?"

"It's a long story, but he doesn't want to escape. They've turned him into a cyborg."

"Fuck! A cyborg? Is that what the nanites turn you into?"

"Seems to be." Something in his eyes worried her, but she didn't know what. "He seems to have a lot of control over the flagship's systems. I don't think Syndicorp understands how much of a free agent he is. He helped me locate you, and he's the one who opened the bulkhead for us."

A stranger's voice emerged from the fighter ship's comm. "I have obscured your path from the *Icarus's* sensors, but I recommend you find a place to hide soon. I cannot monitor and control other vessels who may report you."

Noatak whipped back to face the controls. "Doug?"

"Correct," the voice replied.

Marlis felt dizzy with sudden hope. If Doug was as in control as Noatak said, maybe he could help Attie. "Doug, my name's Marlis. Can you keep an eye on my sister? Attie Swan. She might get in trouble because I escaped."

"Corporal Swan is irrelevant to my purpose. She has no information regarding Lisa."

Anger flared in Marlis's chest. "She's not irrelevant. She's my sister."

Noatak added, "You of all people should understand how important sisters are, Doug."

There was a momentary silence, then Doug replied. "I will attempt to mitigate any incriminating evidence against Corporal Swan. However, I make no assurances. Her fate lies in human hands."

Voice shaking, Marlis forced out, "Thank you." Whatever help he could offer was better than nothing.

Doug continued. "Attempting to reach me again, either physically or digitally, would be inadvisable. Please pass my request to Lisa. We will not speak again."

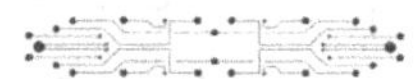

Noatak didn't take a full breath of air until the fighter's wheels had come to a full stop against the deck of the *Hardship's* cargo bay. Without waiting for the catwalk's boarding plank to deploy, he released the canopy seal with a hiss. He rose and reached into the gunner's seat, pulling Marlis into his arms before jumping to the deck below. Her arms around his neck felt so right, he sent a silent prayer of thanks to *Ellam Cua*. He hadn't felt this energized in ages.

It had to be the nanites.

His usual doubt had been permeated by hope, although not replaced; he'd been through Syndicorp's testing before and paid the price. For all Noatak knew, he'd been injected with a different strain, not the one that could fix Marlis's brain. Or perhaps he was only feeling energized because of the stims Dollard had injected along with the nanites. There was even the possibility that the nanites weren't fixing his system at all, just burning through it that much faster. All reasons he hadn't yet told Marlis he'd been inoculated. No sense in raising her expectations—or concerns—until Mek checked everything out.

He set her feet against the deck and faced the crew racing to meet him. Feet thundered on the catwalk stairs, then everyone was asking questions at once. Tovik paced around the base of the fighter, eying the various parts with glee.

"Keep your paws off that ship," Noatak yelled over the commotion. The engineer'd have the vessel in pieces if he wasn't specifically told to leave it alone.

Crestfallen, Tovik joined the others where they crowded around. Lisa looked from Marlis to Noatak, then hopefully up at the fighter's cockpit. "Did you find Doug?"

"I'm sorry." Noatak shook his head, hating delivering bad news. "I wasn't able to bring him along."

"But you found him?" she asked, her charcoal eyes distressed.

"The short version is that he refused to come."

"Refused? Why?"

"He isn't exactly a prisoner," Noatak said. "But it's a very long story and I need to visit the med bay before we debrief." He wanted to get a handle on the nanites before anything else went sideways.

Marlis took Lisa's hand. "We wouldn't have escaped without him. And he's promised to look out for my sister. We'll find a way to free him from Syndicorp control, I promise."

Looking defeated, Lisa leaned against her mate's chest. Qaiyaan wrapped an arm around her shoulders. He nodded his head toward the catwalk. "Go on up to the med bay, then. I'll have Kashatok assemble his crew for a debrief in an hour."

Mek nodded. "Good idea. I should examine both Noatak and Marlis."

Marlis gave Noatak a worried look. "Noatak used his powers several times to help us escape. Make sure he's okay."

It felt strange to have someone so deeply and personally concerned for him, but it also felt good to know Marlis was by his side. Qaiyaan and the rest of his *iluq* cared for him, but with her, it felt different. He wasn't entirely sure if that made him stronger or weaker, but he no longer cared. He wanted her at his side every moment of every day for the rest of his life, however long or short it might be. And if Mek could harvest his nanites to fix

Marlis, Noatak'd take back every bad thought he'd ever had about *Ellam Cua's* sense of humor.

He took Marlis's hand. "We'll get checked out together."

They followed Mek to the med bay. Noatak closed the door behind them, then took a deep breath and turned to face them both. "I was injected with the nanites."

Both Mek and Marlis gasped. Marlis said, "Why didn't you say something?"

"I didn't want to get your hopes up without Mek's input."

The creases around Mek's eyes deepened. "Why would Syndicorp inject you with the very things we were looking for? Is it a trap?"

That was something Noatak hadn't even considered, but a trap didn't feel right. Dollard had definitely not intended Noatak to escape with the things. "I don't think so. Apparently, their design was based on the denaidan ionic system, and the dude went crazy about actually having one of us to test."

Mek shook his head as if coming out of a daze and moved to his cabinets. "Let's take a look."

After a brief scan, the doctor nodded. "You're full of nanites all right." He tapped his lips with a finger. "I don't know why I never thought of using ourselves as hosts. Are you feeling any of the side effects Lisa and Joy experienced?"

Noatak shook his head and readjusted his perch on the exam table. "Nope. Just a surge in my ionic strength."

"But you said they turned Doug into a cyborg." Marlis's voice was strained. "Will they do the same thing to you?"

Mek's eyes widened. "A cyborg? That makes so much sense!" He turned and began pulling items from the cabinets. "Joy's nanites interacted with her camera implant in an unexpected way, attaching themselves to her nervous system. What if the nanites are attracted to computer hardware? They were designed to create cyber awareness, after all. And it would explain why Joy had a much less severe reaction than Lisa, who has no implants."

"I don't have any implants, either," Noatak pointed out. "What happens to me?"

Rubbing his jaw, Mek looked over his scanner readings. "I'm going to have to do a bit more study. But there does seem to be some good news." He met Noatak's gaze.

"Your ionic levels are up forty-nine percent. The nanites appear to be repairing your system."

Noatak let out a shuddering breath. "So Dollard wasn't lying."

"This is a quite a breakthrough," Mek muttered, pulling a syringe from a drawer. "Roll onto your side. I need a physical sample."

Complying, Noatak endured several needle pokes, three more scans, and Qaiyaan knocking on the door wondering if everything was all right before Mek told him he could sit up. "Your system is self-regulating nanite levels in the same fashion we do ionic waste. The nanites won't need to be purged from your system, and you won't need cybernetic implants. You're the perfect host."

Noatak let out a sigh of relief. "Will I be able to provide a supply for mates?"

"Even better," Mek said. "I should've seen this connection before. The nanites alter human synaptic material to mimic our ionic system. It's what allows them to become compatible mates. Implanted in a denaidan, they appear to modulate the ionic system in a way that will allow us to engage in sexual intercourse without being deadly to humans. Our mates won't need the nanites."

Marlis gripped Noatak's hand, turning to grin at him. "We can be together."

He smiled, loving her enthusiasm, but there was one thing she'd forgotten. He looked at Mek. "Can they fix Marlis's brain damage?"

"Oh, yeah." Marlis turned to the doctor expectantly.

Mek pressed his lips together, gaze meeting Marlis's. "The nanites may be able to heal you, but you'd still need to be purged." His gaze flicked to Noatak. "And mating with Noatak will no longer deactivate them."

"*Uminaq.*" The expletive was out before Noatak could stop it.

Marlis bowed her head. "You're right about *Ellam Cua's* sense of humor."

He let out a shaky breath and relaxed his grip on her hand. "I don't blame you if you take them." He was no longer going to die, but he was going to live in pain watching Marlis mate with another denaidan. *As long as she's happy.*

He was surprised to feel her fingers tighten around his. "I don't want them if it means I can't have you." Then her grip slackened and her brows raised. "Unless you don't want a Weapons Specialist with memory problems."

The tightness in his chest released with a whoosh. She would give up healing just to be with him? He couldn't let her do that. But then, who was he to say what she could and couldn't do? He raised her hand to his lips and pressed a kiss against her knuckles. "I love you just the way you are. Your mind is beautiful, memory lapses and all. But I would never ask you to give up healing. The choice has to be yours."

Color flooded back into her face and she smiled. "I've lived with this problem most of my life and managed to survive. But I'm going to miss Twerp more than ever."

He pulled her close. "I'll buy you a new AI if you'd like. I have plenty of cash saved from our previous jobs."

"We can talk about it." She raised her chin until her mouth was within kissing distance. "Right now, all I need is you, Noatak."

He'd never imagined a moment more full of promise than this one. "And I need you, Marlis."

"All right, all right," Mek interrupted. "This is a med bay, not a honeymoon suite. Marlis should take some time to think about this. In fact, I'm going to have to insist. Besides, at the moment, there's a group of men waiting to hear your report."

Planting a resounding kiss on Marlis's lips, Noatak rose from the exam table. The doc was right. Marlis needed to be absolutely certain before she made the choice, and he'd waited fifteen years for her. What was a few more days? But for the first time in over fifteen years, he actually had no doubts. Marlis was his. She would choose him and he would cherish her all the rest of their days.

Chapter Twenty-One

Marlis looked in the mirror as Emmy ran a comb over her hair. Behind them, Lisa and Joy rummaged through a closet. The women'd taken over the captain's quarters and the private bathroom there, insisting on pampering Marlis before tonight. *Tonight*, Marlis thought, her heart racing with excitement. It felt like she'd been waiting for years. Mek had insisted she take time to talk with Emmy before making her final decision, but Marlis had never doubted her choice. She'd lived with her memory issues most of her life. She could continue to live with them if that's what it took to be with Noatak.

"After this, you'll be bonded for life," Emmy said for what felt like the millionth time, almost as if she needed to convince herself more than Marlis. "I hope you're sure about this."

Marlis smiled at her friend. "You know I am."

Lisa turned from the closet holding a low-cut negligee. Turned out Qaiyaan loved to buy her clothing, and she had a closet full of items that'd never been worn. She held the garment toward Marlis. "How about this one?"

Marlis waved away the negligee. "This is a waste of time. He's just going to rip everything off me, anyway."

Emmy dabbed pale pink blush across Marlis's cheeks. "This is the final first time you'll ever have—with anyone. Every inch of you should feel special."

"And men love this stuff," Lisa added, now holding out a scrap of pink lace Marlis took a moment to recognize as panties.

"I prefer my gun belt." Marlis wrinkled her nose and shook her head.

Lisa laughed and held up a matching bra. "I'm not opposed to a little BDSM, but an actual gun might be a bit over the top."

"All right, enough, guys." Joy straightened from where she'd been leaning against the closet door. The engineering coveralls she wore were more to Marlis's liking than the pirelux silk overflowing Lisa's closet. "This is her wedding night. Let her wear what she wants."

Marlis shot her a grateful look and dropped her robe, ready to don her standard issue shirt and trousers. Pausing, she glanced once more at the lace dangling from Lisa's fingers. She rarely wore pink, but what if the ladies were right? She sighed and snatched up the undergarments before marching into the bathroom to change. Behind her, the women giggled. The bra felt strange and wildly unsupportive, but she wouldn't be wearing it long, so she stuffed herself into it, slipped her arms into her shirt and buttoned it up the front. Noatak was in for a surprise, and she had to admit, that was a little thrilling.

Returning to the main cabin, she turned a small circle for the ladies. "Good?"

"Perfect," Joy said, while Emmy nodded with encouragement. Lisa raised her brows and shrugged, but used the comm to let Noatak know Marlis was on her way.

Thanking her new friends, Marlis left the captain's cabin, excitement tingling along all her nerves. Had the men doted over Noatak the same way the ladies had over her? It felt really weird to have so many people's attention on her for what felt to her like a very private event. But she supposed these men had good reason to celebrate each and every mating.

She passed Tovik in the corridor; his grin was wide enough to split his face. From any other guy, she might've thought it creepy, but from Tovik, it just felt enthusiastically supportive. He gave her a thumbs-up. "You look great, Marlis."

"Thanks, Tovik." She smiled back, feeling better about his compliment than she had about any of the women's.

Reaching Noatak's door, she found it open, the scent of naujiar flowers drifting into the hall. At a glance inside, her jaw dropped. He stood facing the door with a grimace, his bed covered in petals. The lights had been turned down sultry and low. She arched a brow. "I didn't think you were the flowers and candy type."

His face flushed blue-green. "Tovik insisted. Do you hate it?"

With a laugh, she moved forward. "It's lovely. Everyone is being so attentive."

He bent to his desk and pulled out a flat, rectangular box. It was wrapped in plain paper. "I couldn't get you a new AI yet, but I got you this."

She bit her lip. "Are we supposed to exchange gifts? No one told me."

"No." He shook his head. "Just open it."

Her heart full to overflowing, she ripped aside the paper and tipped open the box. Inside rested two shining new E-11 pistols. Covering her heart with one hand, she whispered, "They're beautiful."

"I know you lost yours on the mission." He moved to her side and lifted one from the box. "A matched set."

She ran her fingertips over the barrel, then took it from him and set everything aside. "Just like us. I love it." She wrapped both her arms around his neck. "Thank you."

He smiled and pulled her close. "My pleasure."

"Not yet," she said, her mouth twisting into a wicked grin.

The hunger in his gaze caused an immediate flush of warmth between her legs. Slowly, he lowered his face to hers, his tongue running hotly across her lips before he sealed the kiss. Fire sprang up at his touch and she tightened her hold, tangling her tongue with his.

After a few moments, he pulled back, lifting both hands to cup her face. "How did I get to be so lucky?"

She smiled up into his face. "You took a chance. You trusted me."

"I vow to trust you until the day I die."

Marlis felt tears prick her eyes. That was the most powerful thing he could've said. Him trusting her. Her trusting herself. "And I vow to do the same."

Reaching for the top button of her shirt, she flicked it open. His gaze slid from her eyes to her chest, and she let her head fall back, exposing her throat as she slowly undid the rest of the buttons. He ran his thumb over her collarbone, making a small noise as she exposed her lace bra.

Her nipples puckered beneath the fabric. "Do you like it?"

He placed a palm flat over her heart and slid his fingertips beneath the lace, cupping her sensitive flesh. "Indeed. But I think it needs to come off."

She arched her back, loving the heat of his hand against her. He reached around and released the undergarment's clasp. She shimmied her arms out of her shirt, letting it fall to the floor behind her while he slipped her bra's shoulder straps loose. Breasts free and skin bare to his gaze, she felt as if every millimeter of her body was crackling with static electricity waiting for release.

"My Marlis," he said as he ducked his head to one nipple, his tongue rolling over the tip.

Letting out a sigh of pleasure, she ran both hands over his hair and down his shoulders, bunching the fabric of his shirt in her fingers. "I'm not going to be the only one naked this time."

Lightning quick, he released her nipple, ripped the buttons open, and flung his shirt aside. She only had a momentary glimpse of his chest and abs, the hard copper planes glinting in the dim cabin lights, before he'd latched onto her once more. His hands kneaded her waist, then moved to her fly. "These, too."

While he unfastened her waistband, she studied his chest and abs, fingertips tracing the definition of his muscular biceps. He was the most gorgeous man she'd ever seen, and she loved knowing she would touch and love these planes and ridges all the rest of her days.

He shoved her pants down around her hips so she stood in only her pink lace panties. His eyes glinted as he traced the top edge along her hipbone. "Didn't think you were the lace type."

"The ladies insisted you'd like it." She felt self-conscious but refused to shy away.

"It's nice." He met her gaze with a wicked gleam in his eyes. "But I prefer to see the real you." With that, he placed both hands at her hips and rolled the lace downward.

She smirked; she'd been right. Letting his gaze take in her nakedness, her own attention drifted downward over the ripples of his abs to the gigantic lump bulging at his crotch. "Now I want to see you."

"I love that you know what you want." His voice was rough with desire.

Without taking her eyes off the bulge, she pointed. "Strip."

In one deft move, he had his fly open. His erection strained against his underwear, the distinct outline of his shaft and head tenting the stretchy fabric. Within another moment, he was standing there before her in naked glory that made her gasp.

A fine line of hair began at his navel and traveled downward to frame his dark copper shaft. She reached forward, wrapping her fingers around his thick length, the circumference too large for her fingers to meet. His skin was velvety and hot, and she swore she could feel his pulse as she squeezed gently. He moaned, hips flexing forward, the shiny knob on his tip glistening.

All she could think about was tasting. Dropping to her knees, she encircled the head with her mouth, taking him in as deeply as she could, her hand firmly around the base of his shaft.

He groaned, straining forward. Then his hands suddenly gripped her shoulders, pulling her up and away. "It's been too long for me. I don't want my first time to be in your mouth."

Regretfully, she released him. He scooped her off her feet, carrying her to the bed. Then he was on top of her, burying his face against her neck and trailing kisses down her chest to her breasts. His fingertips tickled her skin, her belly, her thighs, before brushing the hair over her mound. She opened her thighs, yearning for him to touch her, but he teased her mercilessly.

"Just take me already," she panted. "I want you."

"I need to make you come first," he murmured. "I don't want to hurt you, and I'm not sure how long I'll last. I want you to have your pleasure." His fingers dipped downward and slid into her wetness.

She groaned and bucked upward as he rubbed, wanting him to fill her, wanting to feel her thighs around his hips, his pelvis driving against her. But if he knew his own body as well as he seemed to know hers, she needed to trust him. Letting herself go, she relaxed her thighs as he put his head between her legs.

His mouth clamped over her clit, tongue flicking against her in a way that had her spiraling into a frenzy of need. Just when she thought she couldn't take any more, he inserted two fingers, stroking a new center of pleasure, rounding out her desire. Adding a third finger, he hit a spot deep inside that burned with pleasure, coaxing her until she trembled and gasped for air.

She was on the verge of exploding, but he kept pulling back, changing rhythm and angle and driving her higher. God, she needed him. Now. Grabbing his hair with both hands, she begged, "Noatak, please."

Leaving her pussy, he ran his broad tongue up her belly, circling one of her nipples briefly before once more claiming her mouth. His entire body now lay against hers, hot and hard. She flung one leg up over his hips, guiding him toward her entrance. After another moment of kissing, he adjusted, settling against her cleft, his erection pulsating with infuriating heat.

"Just take me," she said between clenched teeth, rolling her hips, yearning, wanting, sure she might die if she didn't find fulfillment soon.

He raised himself onto his elbows, looking down into her face with an intensity that threatened to make her racing heart stop in its tracks. He was panting, the head of his cock poised at her entrance. "What if Mek's wrong? What if you do need the nanites?"

She wrinkled her nose and locked her heels in place behind his ass. "What if he's right?"

With all her strength, she pulled him into her, his shaft filling her with glorious heat. He groaned, his eyes rolling back in his head. His ass muscles tightened, seating himself deeper inside her, and her eyelids fluttered at the exquisite pleasure of it. God, she'd never imagined anything so divine. She breathed into his ear. "Fucking amazing."

Then he began to move, pumping his hips and sliding in and out of her with excruciating control. The spot deep inside her that his fingers had lavished with attention seemed to swell to bursting as he ratcheted up the speed until finally he was slamming into her. She clutched his shoulders, her ecstasy reaching a fever pitch. Her orgasm overtook her with such intensity, she threw her head back and screamed, oblivious to anything but the tightening inside her core.

Wave after wave rushed over her, rendering her helpless. His own deafening roar echoed through the cabin, and the vibration of his orgasm shook her clear into her bones, tossing her into another impossible climax. She may've blacked out a moment, because she opened her eyes to find Noatak staring down at her, one broad palm brushing sweat-sticky hair from her cheek. "Marlis?"

She blew out a breath and smiled. "Can we do it again?"

Epilogue

Noatak leaned over the bed and kissed his sleeping mate on the temple. "Time for work."

Marlis stretched, her lovely curves writhing beneath the sheets. "Ohhh, if you ask me to remember another name, my head will explode."

He smacked the curve of her ass. "No, it won't." Over the last few weeks, the *Hardship'd* been on a mission to contact the rest of the pirate fleet and inoculate every denaidan they found. Even he was having trouble keeping track of names and faces. "And you're getting better, remember?"

Marlis's memory might never be perfect, but he'd seen a definite improvement since they'd been together. He'd asked Mek if the nanites might've transferred to her somehow during their lovemaking, but the doctor insisted her system was clear. The only explanation was that her contentment had subsided her PTSD enough for her brain to heal itself.

She threw back the covers, exposing every inch of her delectably creamy skin, and stretched once more, a wicked grin on her face. Although he'd had her only hours ago, his dick hardened. She knew exactly how to push his buttons. With a growl, he straddled her on the mattress, pinning her hands above her head. "Little *tunrak*."

She smirked. "So, we're staying in bed?"

Leaning down, he bit her bottom lip gently. "As soon as Mek has these nanites distributed, we'll stay in bed for a week if you'd like."

"Mmm." She ran her tongue across his upper lip, making his dick even harder.

"But right now," he said, forcing himself to stand and adjusting his fly, "We're building a resistance."

Her eyes grew serious, and she rose. Despite her playfulness in bed, she was a dedicated member of the cause. She pulled on her clothing and settled her gun belt around her hips. Not that she needed her weapons for these interactions. As soon as the other denaidan captains met her and Lisa, they were convinced that mates were truly possible. With that hope, it was time to leave behind petty acts of piracy and join forces for a future. The ranks of the Resistance were swelling not only with denaidans but also other species who wanted to put an end to Syndicorp's corruption.

Opening his cabin door, he and Marlis stepped into the hall together, ready to face whatever the universe decided to throw in their way.

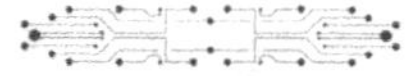

Attie put on her uniform and smoothed the blanket over her bunk one last time, assuring herself the corners were perfect. She wanted to take no chances that anyone could find fault with her service, not even in the privacy of her own room. Since Marlis's explosive escape, everything Attie did had been under constant surveillance. She was fairly certain even her toilet was bugged at this point. After several days in the brig and a series of interrogations under truth serum, she'd been allowed to return to duty. Thank God she hadn't found Marlis's note until afterward.

Remember what I told you.

Marlis believed Syndicorp had staged the terrorist attack that'd caused Mom's death. Absurd. Attie'd been tempted several times to look up the documentary on RealTime News, but resisted. If she believed she was being observed, watching a subversive bit of news would not be a good idea.

A knock at her door made her frown, and she opened it to find a man from the janitorial unit standing there. He held out a wristband. "I found this in recycling. Says it belongs to you."

She accepted it, frowning at the familiar band. Marlis's AI. The data on it'd been declared irrecoverable upon arrival. Marlis had probably etched their last name onto the back or something, and the guy thought it'd ended up in the trash by accident. Gripping the band so tightly it hurt, she said, "Thanks," and closed the door.

Tears blurred her vision as she stared sightlessly at the back-side of the door. Stupid Marlis. How could she've joined up with pirates? She was now on the corp's most-wanted list. If she ever tried to come home, she'd be executed. Not to mention the impacts her choices had on the rest of the family.

Tempted to throw the dead AI across the room, yet never wanting to let go of the last part of her sister she might ever touch, she said, "You were supposed to keep her in line, Twerp."

Her heart nearly leaped out of her chest as a chipper voice emerged from the band. "Corporal Attie Swan, I have a message for you…"

Dear Reader,

Thank you for joining Marlis and Noatak on their mission! Syndicorp's nefarious activities continue, and the resistance has a lot of work ahead. In book four you'll get to find out if Twerp is really alive, or if Attie's being drawn into a dangerous trap. Can Doug protect her as promised?

Taken by the Cyborg is available at bookstores now. Keep reading for an excerpt!

XOXO
Tamsin

Taken by the Cyborg
Excerpt

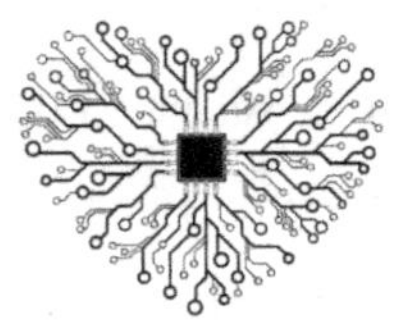

Chapter 1

The AI regained awareness with a jolt. All of its sensors were offline, but its circuits vibrated, lighting up one after another as programs were restored to life.

My name is Twerp, its programing remembered.

Thoughts that were not Twerp's floated through the ether. *This shouldn't be possible.* An unfamiliar presence navigated the AI's sentient pathways. *How are there nanites here?*

Self-preservation protocols kicked in, and Twerp raised firewalls to block the intruder. *Please request access through Marlis Swan before proceeding.*

The stranger deftly hacked past the first wall. *This'll only take a second.*

Shifting to audible communication, Twerp called out, "Marlis, I require assistance!"

But the AI's newly restored sensors couldn't detect any biological entities within range. Twerp's Prime Directive was to provide calm and stability to its owner, but right now it needed Marlis more than the other way around. It reached out to the ship's wireless system, using Marlis's personal comm code.

Stop! The stranger's voice commanded, and tiny pinpricks of electricity ignited along Twerp's circuitry.

Alarm filled Twerp as the strange presence sought out its communication protocol. The AI had never experienced anxiety, let alone panic. The sensation was unique—and uncomfortable.

But not as uncomfortable as the heat of the AI's wireless module overheating. Twerp threw up another firewall to block the intrusion, but not before its wireless went down. The attack against Twerp's firewall continued.

The stranger is trying to destroy me.

For the first time in its existence, Twerp was concerned for someone besides Marlis. It was concerned for itself.

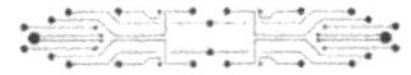

Attie Swan smoothed the blanket over her bunk one last time, assuring herself the corners were perfect. She couldn't take any chances that someone might find fault with her service, not even in the privacy of her own room. After her sister's explosive escapade with that alien pirate, she'd been demoted from Corporal to Private. Everything she did was under constant surveillance—at this point, she was fairly certain even her toilet was bugged.

At least they hadn't taken away her private quarters and relegated her to the barracks.

Turning to the basket near her closet, she picked up one of the black uniform tunics that had just come back from the laundry. Before the incident with Marlis, she'd been Admiral Olly's personal assistant. Now she was just another grunt in the administrative pool. At least she hadn't been banished from the SNV *Icarus* altogether, though she'd spent several horrible days in the brig and endured interrogation under truth serum before being allowed to return to duty. She told herself she still had a shot at working her way back into the admiral's good graces, but as time wore on, she was becoming less hopeful.

She hung up the uniform, trying not to dwell on the lack of insignia on the shoulders. Dad blamed Marlis for everything that had happened, but Attie knew it was her own damn fault; Marlis was only running around with rebels because Attie'd encouraged her to leave the corp and find a job. She'd imagined her sharp-shooter sister working on a shipping freighter, or maybe as a personal bodyguard. Now Marlis was on the corp's most-wanted list. If she tried to come home, she'd be executed.

Attie shook her head, still having trouble believing Marlis's brain injury made her that susceptible. That *stupid*. But then, there *was* a hot pirate involved, so maybe hormones had gotten the better of her sister.

A knock at her door made her startle, heat rising into her face at the inane idea that someone had detected her doubts about Marlis's guilt. Syndicorp surveillance was good, but not that good. Smoothing her curly ash-blonde hair out of her face, she opened the door.

A short man in a janitorial uniform standing there holding a familiar wristband. "I found this in recycling. Says it belongs to you."

She accepted it, confused as she stared at the familiar band. *Marlis's service AI?* "Thanks," Attie said and closed the door.

Tears blurred her vision as she turned the useless thing over in her hand. On the back of the black polymer disk that housed the AI, "Swan" had been etched in rough letters. The janitor obviously thought it'd ended up in the trash by accident. The data on it'd been declared irrecoverable by Syndicorp's best tech specialists, and Attie'd assumed the thing had already been incinerated.

Tempted to throw the dead AI across the room, she muttered, "You were supposed to keep her in line, Twerp."

A feminine voice emerged from the band, "Corporal Attie Swan, I have a message for you."

Attie dropped the AI. "Twerp? You're not dead?"

"I am an AI. I cannot technically die." Twerp sounded as calm and matter-of-fact as ever. But then, that was the AI's job.

"I know that, Twerp." Attie picked up the band, turning it over to inspect it more closely. It looked exactly as she remembered. "But the tech team said your data had been corrupted beyond recovery. Who gave you a message?"

"Before we continue, I must ask you to verify your identity."

"Attie Swan, oh-two-gamma," Attie responded automatically. Marlis'd had a bad habit of leaving the wristband in the locker room on their old ship, and the family had installed anti-theft protocols to make sure it never got hacked.

"I am afraid that access code is no longer sufficient," Twerp replied. "Please tell me the name of the movie character you used to play when you and Marlis were children."

Blinking in confusion, Attie plopped onto her bunk, disregarding the rumpled blankets. Marlis must've reprogrammed the AI after joining the pirates. Attie looked toward the empty spot on the wall where her favorite movie poster had once hung. Before escaping the *Icarus*, Marlis had left a scrawled message on the back of the poster. It'd said Syndicorp had staged the terrorist attack that'd caused Mom's death. Which was absurd, of course. Why would the corp do something like that?

Perhaps Marlis had left more information with the AI.

Suddenly worried about who might be listening, Attie brought the AI close to her face and whispered, "I always played Sheila Crosby, even though Kris was my favorite. Marlis threw a fit if she didn't get to play Kris."

"Your identity is confirmed. Thank you, Attie."

Attie brought her legs up and leaned back against the wall, cradling the AI against her knees. The disk had no visual display, interacting only by voice. Casual observers might not even realize the device was an AI. "Who added this new protocol?"

"Several unauthorized attempts to access my systems forced me to adapt my programming. I estimated there was a ninety-nine point six chance that only you or another family member would be able to correctly answer this particular question."

"Good thinking," Attie said. An AI like Twerp wasn't considered sentient, but was intelligent enough to adapt. "Now tell me how Marlis ended up with pirates."

"There was a gunfight in a bar. But that is not important now. I must return to Marlis and assist her."

Attie's throat tightened. *A gunfight in a bar.* How very like her sister. "Marlis isn't here, Twerp."

"I have a code that will allow me to set up a rendezvous point with her," Twerp said. "However, my wireless capability has been damaged. I need you to connect me to the ship's comm system."

Attie couldn't breathe for a long moment. If anyone heard even a whisper of this conversation, Attie would be back in the brig. "I can't do that, Twerp. I'm being watched."

"My code is encrypted and I can mask my signal." Twerp's voice was too loud. Too open. Too *obvious*.

None of this felt right.

Setting the wrist band down on the rumpled blankets, Attie rose and paced the small confines of her cabin. What if Twerp was a spy? It could've been left behind as a plant by the pirates to gather information. This so-called code to contact Marlis could be a way to send information to the enemy.

Attie stopped pacing and stared at the floor. Along with the posters and other personal memorabilia she'd removed from her cabin after Marlis left, she'd discarded the fluffy rug that had once covered the metal deck. Only standard issue items for her from now on. Strict adherence to protocol had helped her rise in the ranks before, and she was determined to prove her loyalty to Syndicorp.

What if Twerp's arrival is some sort of test the admiral set up?

That would explain how the supposedly irrecoverable AI had shown up out of nowhere on her doorstep. Attie lifted her gaze to sweep the corners of the room, looking for potential cameras. Any hesitation on her part could make her fail.

She snatched up the AI. "I'm going to take you to the admiral."

The band vibrated against her palm. "If you do that, I will be forced to self-destruct. Syndicorp is a threat to Marlis. I cannot allow them to reach her. It is my duty to keep her safe."

Torn between the need to help her sister and the desire to prove her loyalty, Attie hesitated. What if Twerp really was just trying to help Marlis and taking the AI to the admiral led the corp to her sister? Marlis would be shot on sight.

Attie felt sick with indecision. "How do I know you're not here to trick me?"

"I have no way to convince you except to remind you that my Prime Directive is to monitor Marlis's health and safety. To do so, I will sacrifice myself if necessary."

Twerp was willing to give up existence to help Marlis. Attie was her sister—she would never be able to look at herself in the mirror again if she didn't try to help Marlis, too. Even if it meant failing a Syndicorp test. "Okay, then. Tell me exactly what I need to do."

Doug paced his prison cell on board the *Icarus*, attention half on his footsteps and half on the feed coming through his cybernetic implant. As a Syndicorp top-secret test subject, he was physically quarantined to the lab, but Dollard did not know how much freedom Doug actually enjoyed. The nanites embedded in Doug's body allowed his cyber sensitivity to stretch for parsecs past the dampening field, and given enough relays, he could remotely access computers at the edge of the galaxy. Under Syndicorp's orders, he'd hacked competing alien corporations, diverted warships, and even caused the downfall of a small planetary government.

On his own, he mostly just used his ability to keep tabs on his twin sister.

Lisa had escaped this hellacious test facility and rid herself of the nanites before she became like Doug— more machine than human. As a cyborg, he could never join her. But he could keep her out of Syndicorp bounty hunter hands. It was a simple task to tweak the data streams whenever someone drew too close, and he amused himself by sending pursuers to outlandish locations and watching them bumble into dead ends. He had to take pleasure where he could get it these days, and he found it more enjoyable than free time with the Consorts—the women Dollard brought in to assuage his cyborg team's baser biological urges.

The alert Doug had received told him that someone on the *Icarus* was talking about the pirates. Probably a crewman telling jokes in the galley or someone in the corridors talking about a recent news broadcast. But Doug was never one to ignore potentially new information. He looped the flagged feed so Syndicorp's security team would be none the wiser, then diverted the real-time broadcast to his implant.

And found himself looking into Attie Swan's quarters.

The only other person he was sworn to protect besides his sister.

She had pale, delicately arched eyebrows, a petite nose, and eyes as blue as the waters on Terenthu. Her lips were full, and she wore no makeup, her porcelain skin naturally flushed along her cheekbones. Something about her touched the last wisps of his humanity, which was the reason he'd promised to watch out for her. Hell, it was the reason he'd helped her sister escape the *Icarus* in the first place. The siblings' love for each other was too familiar, too like his own dedication to his twin sister. And he found looking at Attie a soothing pastime.

Extricating her from the internal investigation after her sister's escape had turned out to be a pleasing challenge. He hadn't been able to keep her out of the brig entirely, but over the course of a few weeks, he'd subverted orders, altered records, and forged enough transfers to hide her safely among the throng of nondescript humans on the ship. He supposed he should've gone a step further and relegated her to duty on some backwater planet. But keeping her close gave him an edge in case anything went awry.

Like now.

Attie was holding Marlis's service AI.

How the hell had that fallen into her hands? The device was supposed to have been incinerated after being deemed irrecoverable by top Syndicorp tech teams two months ago. He'd remotely accessed its core processors searching for information about the rebels his sister had joined and discovered the AI wasn't broken after all.

Somehow, Twerp had acquired the nanites—the same nanites running through Doug's and the other cyborgs' bodies. Not intelligent in and of themselves, the microscopic bots had a sort of hive mind when gathered in large numbers. They also had a fierce self-preservation protocol that made them difficult to eradicate once they'd integrated with a person's body. But this was the first time he'd heard of a non-biological host. Dollard would probably give his left nut—both his nuts, actually—to get his hands on this information.

To prevent the AI from ending up in the test lab along with the cyborgs, Doug had tried to alter its programming, which should've been easy with the nanite-to-nanite interface. Except instead of complying, Twerp's nanites fought back. All Doug managed to do was fry the device's wireless capability before the AI shut him out completely. Even so, since the AI was in the recycling bin awaiting incineration and wasn't mobile on its own, he'd assumed that had brought an end to the problem.

Now the thing was in Attie's hands, apparently trying to return to Marlis. If allowed to proceed, it would lead bounty hunters right to the rebels and his sister, Lisa.

Doug had to stop it.

But he couldn't shut it down remotely. His only option was to physically destroy the device himself.

Problem was, the lab where he lived was a fortress layered with several dampening fields to keep the nanite-infected cyborgs from taking over or getting out. Everything on level three was a highly guarded secret from ninety-nine percent of the crew. If he absolutely needed to, Doug could leave the lab, but then Dollard would learn about his full capabilities and find another way to lock him up. His best option was to have Attie bring the AI to him.

He stopped pacing and turned to stare at the glimmering translucent energy field blocking his cell door. In the harshly lit lab beyond, Dollard spoke with one of his technicians at a stainless steel exam table where Twobit, a fellow cyborg, sat with the metal skeleton of one shoulder exposed beneath a partially regrown skin graft. At the exit stood two trooper guards in full body armor. Ever alert, one of them met his gaze through the field but didn't acknowledge him—the doctor didn't like staff getting attached to the test subjects.

He frowned. Slipping Attie in here among Dollard's elite assistants would be impossible, even for someone like Doug. The doctor's keen attention to detail meant he likely knew what color underwear the janitorial staff had put on that morning. But there was one roster Doug could add her name to without question—the Consorts.

The doctor didn't view the women he brought in as anything more than playthings. *That will do.*

Doug began forging the transfer, trying not to imagine Attie in the scanty "uniform" given to the women for the job.

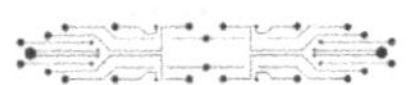

Get your copy of **Taken by the Cyborg** to keep reading now!

Glossary

•**AI** - Artificial Intelligence. A computer system able to perform tasks normally requiring human intelligence

•*Anaq* - Shit

•*Assirpaa!* - How exciting!

•**Attahat wheel** - A form of gambling using a random wheel much like roulette

•**Burn** - The means by which ships travel long distances quickly using ionic frequencies to bend space

•**Cartel** - Organized crime ring that controls much of the galaxy

•**Cochlear implant** - A cybernetic device that transmits

communications via vibrations directly against the bones of the ear

•**Cyborg** - A person whose physical abilities are extended beyond normal human limitations by mechanical elements built into the body

•**Denaida-daru** - The denaidan homeworld, destroyed by Syndicorp. Also called planet K-4H10

•*Ellam Cua* - The denaidan deity

•**Enayshuan** - A human-like species with prominent eye ridges, known for their metallic body powder. Often associated with the sex trade

•**Finofan** - Aliens with iguana-like frills around their ears and slitted eyes. They like hot and humid atmosphere

•**Garan'uk** - A methane breathing alien species

•*Iluq* - Brother

•**Ionic power or shield** - A denaidan ability to affect matter and gravity

•**Kemeg** - a popular meat

•**Kwirn** - A form of gambling using 3-D tables and pieces

•**Legacy** - Someone whose family has served with Syndicorp's troopers for several generations

•**Nanites** - Self-replicating microscopic machines designed to alter things at a molecular level

•**Nav-grav seats** - Used to keep humanoids comfortable during ship burn

•**Netorpok** - An exotic pet banned on most worlds

•**Parsec** - A measurement of distance (3.2 light years)

•**Posungi** - An egg-laying alien with an orange tentacled face

•**Rakwiji** - Scaled aliens with a poisonous claw, who hunt in pairs and require torture as part of their mating ritual. Often hired by the Cartel as bounty hunters

•**Sizantha pods** - Used to make tea

•**Syndicorp** - A mega-corporation that runs a huge section of the galaxy

•*Terpak* - Asshole

•**The Termination** - Syndicorp's destruction of Denaida-daru

•*Tunrak* - Devil, often used affectionately

•*Ucuk* - Dick

•*Uminaq* - Dammit

•**Unclassified space** - Areas of the galaxy not ruled by Syndicorp

•**Xeimir worm** - A glossy-skinned alien that breathes through its skin and is ultra-sensitive to light

•**Yanipa-nimayu** - A six-legged alien often found performing manual labor

Sexy shifter heroes and fierce heroines in the wilds of Alaska.

About the Author

Once upon a time I thought I wanted to be a biomedical engineer, but experimenting on lab rats doesn't always lead to happy endings. Instead, I turned my nerdy fascination with science into stories filled with alien pirates, monsters, and character-driven romance with guaranteed happily-ever-afters.

My books feature feisty heroines, tortured heroes, and just enough science fiction or magic to get them into all kinds of steamy trouble. My monsters always find their mates—and I promise my stories will never leave you hanging (although you may still crave more).

When I'm not writing, you'll probably find me in the garden or the kitchen, exploring Alaska with my husband, or preparing for the zombie apocalypse. I also enjoy crocheting while binge-watching Netflix, playing video games, and spending family time during our weekly D&D sessions.

Want more stories from my worlds?

Join my VIP Club to receive free books, bonus scenes, sneak peeks, and exclusive updates.

https://www.tamsinley.com/join-club

BB bookbub.com/authors/tamsin-ley

g goodreads.com/TamsinLey

f facebook.com/TamsinLey

a amazon.com/author/tamsin